W.  ving

"Author Christine Warren pens a sizzling erotic delight in FANTASY FIX. Bold and daring fantasies of bondage and submission are carefully balanced by loving respect, resulting in an exciting and scorching read."
- *Cynthia Penn, Word Weaving*

"The story is hot. Dmitri's unique mind-reading skill puts an interesting twist on the relationship, while never seeming exploitative."
- *Kristine Kelly, Sensual Romance*

"Ms. Warren's debut novel is a delight. The characters are fun and feisty, with ardent natures."
- *Kristina Smith, Sime~Gen*

Discover for yourself why readers can't get enough of the multiple-award-winning publisher Ellora's Cave. Whether you prefer e-books or paperbacks, be sure to visit EC on the web at www.ellorascave.com for an erotic reading experience that will leave you breathless.

www.ellorascave.com

Ellora's Cave Publishing, Inc.
PO Box 787
Hudson, OH 44236-0787

ISBN # 1-84360-562-7

Fantasy Fix edited by Jennifer Martin.
Cover art by Darrell King.

Warning: The following material contains strong sexual content meant for mature readers. *FANTASY FIX* has been rated NC-17 erotic, by a minimum of three independent reviewers. We strongly suggest storing this book in a place where young readers not meant to view it are unlikely to happen upon it. That said, enjoy…

FANTASY FIX

Written by

CHRISTINE WARREN

Chapter 1

"Good lord, you should have seen her face! I thought her eyes were going to pop right out of her head."

Laughter shook the shoulders of four of the women in the room, while the fifth took the ribbing with good-natured grumping.

"Are you kidding? And miss one second of staring at that *gorgeous* hunk of a man? Our Corinne would never be that stupid." Danice topped off her wine glass from the nearly empty bottle of merlot and grinned slyly. "Besides, if her eyes had popped out, they probably would have just landed on her chin. I think it was on the floor by that point."

Missy laughed. "That accounts for the puddles, then!"

"Hey," Corinne protested with mock dignity, finishing off the white wine in her own glass. "There were no puddles involved. At least, not that early on."

"And they didn't consist of drool anyway," Ava quipped as she selected a chunk of havarti from the plundered plate of cheese on the table in front of her. "I hope those silk sheets of yours didn't stain, Corinne, darling."

"If they did, I don't want to know about it." Regina McNeill laughed and rose from her seat on the floor of her apartment's living room. She thought there might still be a couple of bottles of wine in the kitchen. She might as well break them out. If the company wasn't excuse enough, the damp, dreary spring weather ought to be. "There's such a thing as too much information, you know."

"There is not," Danice shouted at Regina to make sure she'd be heard from the other room. "Friends share everything, Reggie!"

"Mm, especially the dirty parts," Ava purred. Her sleek, dark eyebrows wriggled suggestively and drew another laugh from the group.

Even Reggie laughed while she snagged the last bottle of white from the fridge and another red from off the breakfast bar that separated her tiny kitchen from the rest of her apartment. True to form for the bi-weekly girls' nights, things had gotten raunchy by this stage of the evening. Reggie and her four closest friends had consumed a table full of munchies and more than half a case of wine, and that in only a couple of hours. It was no wonder their conversation had gone straight to the gutter. "I don't get the dirty parts," she commented, bringing the wine with her to the living room and reaching for the corkscrew. "I thought that's what blue movies and romance novels were for."

"We know you don't get the dirty parts." Ava nudged her wine glass toward Reggie and smiled archly. "Which is why I am motioning that you, dear Regina, are going to be our next project."

The suggestion was met with a half-second of silence followed by a rousing cheer from everyone but Reggie.

"Oh, no," Reggie protested, totally forgetting about her struggle with the cork. "I'm not going to be your next victim. Pick someone else." Her eyes had gone wide and nervous, and she shook her head vehemently. Desperate, she looked around at her one-time friends for a way out. "Pick Missy. It ought to be Missy's turn by now…"

"No way, girl. Missy already took a turn." Danice quickly surveyed the room and pursed her lips. "In fact, she's taken two turns. We all have. You are the only one who hasn't yet had even one Fantasy Fix."

"Maybe I'm not broken." Her protests fell on deaf ears, not that she'd expected much else. No one could talk Danice Carter out of an idea, which is why the Fantasy Fixes had gotten off the ground to begin with. Danice had the original brainstorm, with Ava quickly throwing her support behind it, and since the whole thing had been born on another girls' night — complete with its ritual alcohol consumption — Missy and Corinne had quickly jumped onto the bandwagon. Even Reggie had voted to go for it. At the time, she couldn't see the harm. Now she could kick herself.

The Fantasy Fix started when one too many drinks led the conversation to the subject of fantasies — in particular, sexual fantasies.

"Have you ever acted one out?" Ava had wanted to know. "One of the really steamy ones you didn't want anyone to know about?"

Danice scoffed at that. "When would I get the chance? And with who? Reggie's the only one of us with a long-term relationship. I'm lucky if I can get lucky, let alone find a guy to act out the good stuff with."

"I don't know if that makes Reggie lucky though," Corinne observed. "Sometimes it's even harder to do the fantasy thing with a real partner than it would be with someone you don't know as well. There's more at stake. Personally, if I'm going to admit I want to dress up in red leather and have some hunk call me Mistress, I think I'd rather do it with a stranger."

"Mistress, huh?" Missy giggled and grinned. "You go, girl. I wouldn't have pegged you for it, but I think I like this side of you. You're right though; strangers would be easier."

"Exactly," Danice agreed. "Besides, you pull out the big guns with a lover, and he's gonna want in on the fantasizing. Lovers want to get inside your head. At least if you were doing the fantasy thing with a stranger, you can do it all the way, not worry about him whining that *he* wants to be the Emperor this time."

They had all laughed, except for Ava. She'd had that look.

"You know, Corinne," she said slowly, "I know someone, a real hunk, who would love the opportunity to call someone mistress without paying for it or doing the long-term thing. I could maybe hook you two up."

Missy laughed. "Playing matchmaker, Ava? You know, I've been looking for a nice mountain man to kidnap me and keep me in his cabin for a weekend or two. Know anyone like that?"

"I don't know about Ava, but I do," Danice chimed in. "I could fix you up with that fantasy. In fact, I bet if we put our heads together, we could maybe help each other out. All five of us. I bet we could come up with a way for any four of us to fix up the other one. Make it possible for her to live her fantasies. Give her a Fantasy Fix."

That had been the beginning of the end. A vote had revealed the five of them to be just drunk enough and just insane enough to agree to help each other find a way to live out their fantasies. They'd drawn up a plan, collected five fantasies from each member of the group and plunged headfirst into round one. By putting their heads together, the five friends found they knew an awful lot of men who fit each other's visions of a fantasy lover. After that, making the arrangements had been easy. Round one had gone off like gangbusters, with each woman taking a turn at acting out one of her five fantasies with one of the eligible bachelors in the Fantasy Pool. Well, each woman had taken a turn except for Reggie.

At the time the idea came together, Reggie had still been seeing Greg, had still been living with Greg, unfortunately, so she'd been exempt. They'd skipped over her, and Reggie had told herself she didn't need a fantasy lover when she had a real one sleeping by her side every night. She hadn't realized that while Greg slept by her side every night, he also fucked his receptionist in his office every afternoon. Their relationship hadn't made it past the beginning of round two. The breakup had been four months ago, and while Reggie had finally reached the stage when she could admit she was better off without the scum-sucker, she still didn't quite feel ready for a Fantasy Fix.

Of course, try to tell that to her friends.

And she was. She was trying really, really hard. They just refused to listen.

"Get the hat," Danice instructed Missy while Corinne took the bottle of wine from Reggie's hands and finished opening it. "Who's got custody of Ms. McNeill's fantasies?"

Four women looked at each other, and Reggie had the fleeting hope her fantasies had been lost to the ether, and they could just forget this whole insane idea.

"I didn't bring them," Missy admitted. "I didn't know Corinne was finished, so I didn't think we'd be drawing tonight."

Reggie started to grin.

"No matter," Ava dismissed. "Just get a pen and paper. She can draw up five new ones. Knowing our bashful and generally monogamous friend, her old ones probably all featured the Slimeball, anyway."

Reggie felt the first stirrings of panic. Her friends had never liked Greg—neither did Reggie these days—but that didn't mean she felt ready to hop into bed with a stranger.

"You know, I really think—"

"That you need to make these good, girl," Danice interrupted firmly, handing Reggie a pad and a pen. "Now is your chance to live it up. Get fantasizing."

Missy returned to the group and held up the straw hat she had snagged from Reggie's hall closet. "Who's going to draw?"

"I will," Corinne offered and set her refilled wineglass on the cocktail table. "Since I had the last Fix."

Reggie felt her already nebulous control over her own fate slipping permanently from her grasp. "Wait a minute, guys. I'm not so sure this is really a good idea. Maybe I'm not ready for this. Maybe I need to finish getting over this thing with Greg—"

"Trust me when I tell you, darling, the best way to get over that asshole is to fuck him right out of your memory." Trust Ava to lay it all out in black and white. She never had been one to beat around the bush. "And since I don't see you going out and picking up an assistant to help you with that, it is up to your friends to pick one up for you."

"But—"

"Plant it, Reg." Danice pushed Reggie down onto the sofa and handed her a large glass of wine. "It's your turn, and you are not backing out this time."

Reggie didn't even get the chance to launch another argument before Corinne took a turn with the browbeating. "No more stalling. You had your chance to veto this Fix in the beginning just like we all did, but once you threw in your fantasies, and we started round one, you were committed."

Reggie scowled. "I ought to be committed."

"Actually, that's a really good point," Missy interrupted. "She was in this beginning with round one, right? But she never got a turn. So I think," she paused to grin at the other women, "Reggie should get a double draw. Two fantasies for the price of one, so to speak."

"Yes!" Danice's exclamation overrode Reggie's protest. "It'll be our job as the Fixers to find a way to fit the two fantasies together. Don't worry, toots. We'll find a way to make it happen for you."

"Absolutely."

"It'll be great."

"Just trust us."

Reggie figured that meant she was doomed, but looking at the solid wall of sisterly unity in front of her, she also figured resistance would prove futile. She was right.

"Write!" Ava ordered, pointing imperiously at the blank paper on Reggie's lap. "We need five fantasies, Ms. McNeill, the kinkier the better."

"But—"

"No buts. Concentrate on butts." Corinne grinned. "And pecs and abs and cocks. And really talented hands."

They all laughed, and Reggie knew her reprieve had come to an ignominious end. She could never get away without listing five fantasies and throwing them—and herself—on her friends' non-existent mercy.

"I don't see the pen moving, Reg," Missy teased her, waggling her eyebrows. "Get going. This is your chance to do all the things you weren't sure were even physically possible."

Reggie started to snap back she'd prefer the impossible, but she stopped when a thought occurred to her. She pursed her lips and tapped the pen against the pad. "So were there any rules about these fantasies? I can't remember all the particulars we decided on. I think I was too drunk."

"Anything goes, baby." Danice grinned. "You can ask for anything you want, and if we can't get it for you, we have to pay the forfeit. One month of celibacy each."

"Which is not going to be a problem, darling. We can get you anything you want, Regina, so quit stalling and write."

Reggie narrowed her eyes and obeyed Ava's command. She knew she was being vindictive with the first four slips of paper she filled out, but she didn't find this little stunt amusing, and she found the insistence of her friends more than a little annoying. As far as she could tell, a month of abstinence would be good for them. Maybe it would get their mind off sex for sixty consecutive seconds.

Fighting back a grin, Reggie quickly scribbled out four fantasies, each impossible for anyone to fulfill, even her

14

resourceful friends...unless they could manage to find a vampire, an alien, Bigfoot or Elvis, still alive, in shape and fully functional. She still had to come up with one more, though, and she'd just run out of *Weekly World News* headlines.

"Oh, you cannot tell me you don't have enough fantasies," Danice said, planting a hand on her hip and glaring down at Reggie while the other woman struggled to think of a final impossible request. "You are twenty-seven years old, girl, and the last two, you spent chained to Groping Gregory. You got time to make up for!"

"I'm thinking."

"Don't think," Ava ordered, holding out the hat. "Fantasize. Now."

Reggie rolled her eyes. Now they were giving her a deadline. She wracked her brain for another ten seconds and came up blank, but when even soft-hearted Missy started in on her to finish, she dashed off the first thing that came to her mind and tossed the five folded slips of paper into the hat. The last one really *was* one of her fantasies, but the chances of it being drawn weren't good, so if the gods loved her, it would never see the light of day. She'd be cuddling a yeti before it ever happened.

The thought almost made her grin, but she didn't want to make the others suspicious. If she gave up too readily now, they'd suspect something, and they'd make her come up with some plausible scenarios. She pasted a scowl on her face and pretended to bear a big grudge. "Fine. I give up! Do your worst," Reggie growled, as if she had no intention of apologizing. She drained her wine glass while her friends whooped their glee, then she reached for the bottle of merlot and poured another.

Corinne settled down on the couch beside Reggie and patted her knee companionably. "Buck up, grasshopper. We love you, and I can guarantee that we will give you one hell of a Fix."

"That's what I'm afraid of."

"All right, ladies." Ava stood in front of the coffee table with Reggie's hat in her hand and a gleeful smile on her face. "If I may have your attention, let's get started, since our Fix for this draw is already a bit behind the rest of us. Corinne, if you'd care to do the honors? Remember, we need a double draw for Ms. McNeill."

Corinne grinned and leaned forward to reach into the hat Ava held just above their heads. "Can I get a drum roll, please?"

Danice banged her hands on the edge of the coffee table. *As if I don't already have a headache*, Reggie thought, crossing her arms and tucking her chin to her chest like a petulant two-year-old, all the while fighting to keep her lips from sliding into a grin.

With a flourish, Corinne drew two slips of white paper from the inside of the hat and rubbed them together like a couple of crisp twenties before handing them off to Ava. "The envelope, ma'am."

"Thank you, Corinne, darling. Now, what do we have here?"

The other three women leaned closer while Reggie appeared to sulk into her merlot.

"Let's hear it!"

"Come on, what's it say?"

"I bet it's kinky. The quiet ones are always into kinky."

Ava ignored them while she read…while one carefully sculpted eyebrow arched into a perfect bow…while her lips pursed…while she whistled long and low.

"I knew it!" Corinne blurt out, punching the air in emphasis. "I told you it's the quiet ones."

"You have no idea," Ava purred, finally looking up to see Reggie turning a peculiar shade of magenta. "Why, Regina Elaina McNeill, I am shocked. You are quite the little vixen, aren't you?"

"What's it say already?"

Ava smiled. "It says that our dearest friend thought she'd be pulling a fast one on us. Sorry to disappoint you, Regina darling, but you *are* getting Fixed, whether you like it or not."

Missy frowned. "What are you talking about?"

Ava held up one piece of paper and read aloud. "Regina says she wants to be, 'seduced by a sexy, mysterious vampire.'"

Corinne turned a glare on Reggie. "That is not fair, Reg! Your fantasies have to be plausible. You can't hold us responsible for not being able to find you someone who doesn't even exist!"

Reggie wiped the grin off her face, which had appeared when Ava read her fantasy, and prepared to do battle.

"Hush. Don't get your panties in a twist, Corinne, dear," Ava soothed. "You are not destined for celibacy. We will provide Reggie with what she asked for."

Danice rolled her eyes. "You had a few too many glasses of that wine, Ava. Vampires aren't real."

"I know that, and since Regina is perfectly sane—relatively—she knows it as well. If Reggie actually wanted us to find her a genuine vampire, she would be cheating, and I know our friend would never do that. Which means we need to view her fantasy in a more creative light."

"Like how?"

"I'm so glad you asked." Ava purred her answer to Missy's question, but her eyes never wavered from Reggie's. "It just so happens I know of a certain club in the East Village that hosts a regular event on the last Friday of each month. They call it The Vampire Ball."

Corinne laughed. "So we can find Reggie a man there! Since she knows she can't have a real vampire, she'll have to accept a man who could pose as one. Ava, you're brilliant!"

"I try, dear."

"Yeah, you're very trying." Reggie scowled. "I can't believe you're going to pawn me off on some freak who is so out of touch with reality he pretends to be a vampire to get his kicks. That is so pathetic."

Ava's Cheshire cat grin turned steely. "You agreed to the enterprise, Reggie, and you submitted the fantasy. You're bound by the rules just like the rest of us, so unless you want to submit something more realistic, this is the fantasy you get."

"One of them, anyway." Bless her mediating heart; Melissa stepped between the two women before they could come to blows. "What does the other fantasy say? Does she want to be abducted by aliens, or have Elvis's love child?"

Missy tried to joke about it to lighten things up, which Reggie appreciated, but when Ava shook her head and smiled wider, Reggie got nervous.

"Neither," Ava purred, holding up the other slip of paper. "She doesn't want to be Bigfoot's love slave, either."

Oh, no! In that moment, Reggie knew for certain the gods had abandoned her to an ugly fate. She knew which other fantasy Ava had selected. The need to escape suddenly overwhelmed her.

"I need a drink." Reggie pushed off the sofa and attempted to head into the kitchen to hide. She never made it past the end of the coffee table. Danice grabbed her by the shoulders and forced her back to her seat.

"Ah-ah, Reg. Sit your butt back down and prepare to get Fixed."

"Come on, guys. I'm sorry for making up the vampire thing," the victim wailed. "Can't we just forget about it? I'll write a real fantasy this time. I promise. Let's start over. Please?"

"Not a chance. Now that we know you want to be—" Ava consulted the slips of paper, "as you say here, 'seduced and overpowered by a lover,' we are not going to let this go. Especially not when you also have this burning desire to be 'bound, spanked and dominated' by a sexy, commanding brute."

"Oh, wow," Missy breathed, her mouth rounding into an 'o' of surprise, and she stared at her friend through new eyes. "Reggie, I can't believe you never mentioned this. What else have you been keeping secret from us?"

"Nothing," Reggie insisted, though it came out kind of muffled by the hands in which she had buried her flaming face. "Not a damn thing. How could I keep secrets from you people? You're worse than tabloid reporters!"

Danice grinned. "Hey, it's not like you want to get back together with Gregory the Grotesque. Now we just know you're a wild thing in the bedroom. No biggie."

"Oh, not at all." Reggie drained her wine glass and refilled it, taking it with her when she curled into a ball in the corner of her sofa. "Humiliation never killed anyone. I'm sure I'll get over it in another couple of incarnations."

Missy, always the softy, wiped the smile off her face and squeezed Reggie's arm. "Hey, it's not so bad. It's not like you don't know anything embarrassing about any of us. I mean, come on. You know about my mountain man thing. You know Danice got picked up by a marine on shore leave. You know Ava auditioned for a strip show. Let's face it, honey. You're not the only girl out there with…sophisticated tastes."

Seeing their words were maybe beginning to get through to their blushing comrade, Corinne perched on the arm of the sofa beside Reggie and topped off the other woman's drink. "She's right, you know. Besides, we're your best friends. We'd love you even if you had secret fantasies about Dan Quayle. We'd think you were insane, but we'd still love you."

That drew a reluctant smile.

"We would," Danice insisted. "A little kink ain't nothing to be ashamed of, girl. If your fantasies were as vanilla as the rest of you, that's when I'd start to worry."

Ava waved a hand to get their attention. "All true, of course. And, since our reluctantly cooperative friend has two fantasies that work so very well together, I think we can safely assure her that we are going to make sure they come true, and quite quickly, as well. Next week happens to be the last Friday of the month, which means the five of us will be having a very interesting night in the village. If I can propose a toast?"

The women reached for their glasses and held them aloft in anticipation.

"To our dear friend Regina," Ava said after a brief pause. "And to her very own Fantasy Fix. May they be very happy together!"

Chapter Two

Just because the gods had abandoned her to a cruel fate didn't stop Reggie from praying they'd keep her from breaking her ankle.

She took as deep a breath as the black satin corset her friends had laced her into would allow, and concentrated very hard on balancing on her four-inch heels while she descended the steps into the darkened club.

Seven solid days of frantic pleading, threats and attempted bribery had failed to sway Ava or any of the other three women from their determination to "Fix" Reggie. They insisted on making the scheduled trip to the Mausoleum, an unrepentantly Gothic nightclub in the heart of the East Village. None of them had even shown any sympathy for Reggie's pleas, except for Missy.

Even then, as softhearted as she was, Missy refused to side with Reggie against the others. Instead she'd tried to offer reassurance.

"It's not like Ava is really going to pawn you off on a loser, Reg," Missy had said over the phone earlier. "She was just trying to get your goat for giving us such a hard time. She'd kill me if she knew I told you this, but she knows a guy she's been planning to hook you up with forever, and she's having him meet us at the club. I've met him, and he's great. Now will you relax?"

The answer to that, a resounding no of a headache, currently throbbed behind her temples in time to the industrial-techno music that boomed through the loudspeakers. She tried her best to ignore it and stuck like glue to her friends. If she lost them, she'd never find them again in the gyrating throng of identically black-clad bodies. Of course, that went both ways. If she could slip away unnoticed—

A hand clamped over her wrist.

"Stay close!" Ava leaned into their little huddle, but she still had to shout to make herself heard any farther than six inches away. "Let's head over to the bar and get a drink before we plan our attack."

Ava always had been perceptive, and she refused to let go of Reggie while she squeezed and shimmied her way through the crowd toward the black-lit bar at one end of the cavernous room. Reggie figured Ava guessed she'd been planning to bolt.

The women squirmed their way across the dance floor like an amoeba with five pseudopods. Getting up to the bar required the judicious use of a few elbows and an immunity to insults. As the first to reach an empty inch of space, Danice yelled an order for five drinks, and the others closed ranks around Reggie, who promptly rolled her eyes.

"Come on, guys," she protested when they hurried to snag a tall bar table that had just been vacated. "Don't you think you're being just a little paranoid? I'm here. I came. I answered my door when you picked me up instead of refusing to buzz you in. I put on these excuses for clothes you told me to wear. I even let you plant a bag full of sex toys in my closet! I've surrendered. I'm not likely to go anywhere now."

"Because we know you well enough not to trust you," Corinne pointed out, accepting a dark brown beer bottle and taking a moment to survey the crowd. "Ava was the one who thought the corset would be enough to keep you from running. But I brought a leash along just in case."

"Bite me."

"Oh, you'd like that, wouldn't you?"

"Children, please. We have more important things to do than squabble like three year olds. Reggie looks fantastic in her corset, and I'm sure a leash won't be necessary, unless her fantasy wants her to wear one." Ava glanced discreetly at her watch. "We have exactly four hours and fifteen minutes before the party ends and Regina turns back into a pumpkin. Battle stations."

Reggie's four friends faced the four corners of the bar and started scanning for potential partners. Frowning, Reggie leaned close to Missy's ear and spoke in a low murmur, "I thought you said Ava already had someone picked out."

"She does, but she wants you to squirm a little," Missy hissed back, her eyes on the masses of men and women passing before her. "Could you at least look a little nervous? If she knows I warned you, she'll kill me."

Looking nervous would not be a problem. Reggie felt more than a little out of place surrounded by a few hundred twenty-somethings, all of whom seemed to have a genuine fear of sunlight. She hadn't known you could see so many white faces outside of a mime convention.

With a sigh, Reggie scanned the crowd and hoped Ava's friend turned out to be significantly different from any of the men she'd noticed so far.

The crowd really wasn't her type. Most of them were too young for her, and even the ones who were her age or older somehow managed to look like children playing dress up. How could she feel attracted to someone so desperate to escape reality he wished he were a fictional character? She had always preferred her men to have a grip, not that you'd know it from her track record. Take Gregory, for instance. Apparently most of the women in lower Manhattan already had.

Sipping her beer and leaning her elbows on the scarred table, Reggie figured since her friends wanted to do all the work in picking up a man for her tonight, she could indulge in a little brooding over her recent failures.

Greg epitomized her "type," which probably meant she should reevaluate the concept of types. He'd been confident, attractive, intelligent and ambitious, the kind of man mothers all over the world dreamed would walk into their daughters' lives. If her mother hadn't died when Reggie was a kid, she'd probably be calling daily and asking what happened to that charming Greg fellow Reggie used to bring home for holiday visits.

Lisette the Limber had happened, Reggie acknowledged, trying very hard not to picture the little blonde bimbo bent over Greg's desk with her skirt hiked around her waist and her g-string tangled around her ankles. Reggie had been late for her lunch date with Greg and hadn't thought anything about walking right into his office when she saw Lisette's empty desk. She'd thought the woman had been taking a break. Instead, she'd been taking it doggy style from Reggie's fiancé.

Reggie! I can explain!

Had anyone ever invented a more hackneyed reaction to that scene? She'd always credited Greg with a certain level of intelligence, but apparently she'd overestimated him. He might have been a genius when it came to portfolios and earnings ratios, but when it came to facing a shocked lover with his dick hanging out of his pants and his hands all over his administrative assistant, he possessed the approximate smarts of a seven-year old caught throwing snowballs at the poodle next door.

Reggie, I swear, Lisette and I were just —

Screwing like rabid minks on top of the latest NASDAQ reports?

She wished she'd come up with that response at the time, but all she'd been able to do was stand there with her mouth open and her breath frozen in her chest and the hand that wore his ring clenched tightly around the doorknob.

She took another swig of her beer and forced her mind away from replaying the rest of that scene. She still remembered every ugly word they'd hurled back and forth at each other, oblivious to the hallowed reputation of Sterling and Woulk Financial, Inc., but that didn't mean she wanted them echoing in her head right now. Greg's infidelity had ruined her plans for a marriage and family, her trust in the ability of men to keep their promises, and most of her last six months. She'd be damned if she'd let him ruin her night as well.

After drinking her beer on an empty stomach—she'd been too nervous to eat dinner earlier—Reggie could almost see how Ava might have a point. Maybe a good, fantasy-fulfilling fuck *was* the best way to forget about Greg, and if Ava already knew the guy, she could be confident he wouldn't be an axe-murderer or some sort of monster. Maybe she just needed to relax and let herself go with the flow.

Reggie pushed away from the table, and the DJ spun into a new tune. The song had a deep, hypnotic beat and a dark, haunting melody. Reggie signaled for another beer and let her hips pick up the rhythm and sway along with the music. The black leather pants she'd thought would be too confining turned out to move quite well with her shimmies. She ignored the looks her ass attracted from a few men at the bar and tried to locate her friends.

Danice obviously liked the beat, too, because she accepted an invitation to dance with a tall, burly biker and shouted she'd be right back. Reggie watched her go, envying her friend's ease in the crowded club. When her beer came, she raised it to her lips and turned to face the bar. She wondered if she'd be able to pick Ava's friend out of the crowd.

Not the one right in front, she decided, watching a pretty, pale boy gesture grandly to the bevy of emaciated young women who surrounded him. Ava knew Reggie well enough to realize she'd never go for an overly theatrical kid. How in the world would she take someone like that seriously? He'd pull out a pair of handcuffs, and she'd have to ask if his daddy knew where he'd gotten them. She similarly dismissed a handful of brooding punks and a couple of leather-clad biker types. Ava's taste ran to something significantly more sophisticated.

Stubbornly ignoring her headache, she started to think Ava's friend might have stood them up when her gaze hit the end of the bar and skidded to a halt. The most perfect man she'd ever seen sat there in the shadows with a hand wrapped around a glass of amber liquid and his eyes locked directly on her face.

* * * * *

Dmitri Vidâme nursed his single glass of Scotch and wondered yet again how he'd let himself be talked into attending this pretentious little game of make believe. The

"Vampire Ball" hardly fit his normal thinking as to what constituted a good time, and frankly, the attendees who filled the Mausoleum's vast basement dance floor had begun to annoy him.

Look at them, he marveled, struggling to keep the sneer from his face. *If any of these children ever came face to face with a genuine vampire, they'd soil themselves and go running home to mommy.* Barely cut loose from apron strings, and they thought themselves misunderstood and tormented. They thought they felt more comfortable in the dark than in the sunlight, thought they knew what it meant to be isolated and tormented. Dmitri wanted nothing so much as to slap some sense into them.

Actually, that wasn't precisely true. Even more than a little judicious violence, he wanted to go home. A quiet evening in front of his fireplace sounded infinitely more appealing to him than another five minutes surrounded by pretentious children in "gothic" garb. Even one of the endless, politically charged meetings of the Council of Others, on which he sat, sounded more appealing.

He swore under his breath and tossed back half of his drink in one swallow. He'd let Graham, his good friend and fellow Council member, talk him into coming to this torture session. Technically they were supposed to be there on business, looking for the young vamps who had taken to frequenting these Goth events and feeding off the eager attendees. The fledglings risked exposure with their behavior, and the Council had decided they needed a stern warning. He hadn't spotted any of them at this event, though, and he was more than ready to go home. As soon as Graham stopped sniffing around that blowsy little blonde he currently "questioned," Dmitri would say his goodbyes and head out. Maybe he'd stop for a bite on the way home, just to wash the taste of this place out of his mouth.

He had so many better things he could be doing, he reflected, trying to pick Graham out of the shifting crowd. Where had he and that blonde disappeared to? The Council that governed the alliance of New York's vampire and lycanthrope populations had been busy lately, but even those problems hadn't kept his mind occupied. He felt boredom creeping up on him and wondered if it were time for him to step down from his council seat in favor of new pursuits.

Restless, he waited impatiently at the bar, tempted to just forget goodbyes and leave Graham to his fate and his bimbo. He reached for his glass again, and he saw her.

She stepped up to the bar, swept along in the wake of four other women, but Dmitri could not have described a single one of them. He saw only her, with her face like a vision and her body like a gift from the gods.

The woman looked impatient and a little nervous and sadly out of place among the ridiculous throngs that surrounded her. For one thing, she had the look of a woman, rather than a child. He could see she was young, probably in her late twenties, but she wore her age comfortably as a mature woman should. Her skin, milk white and dusted with freckles the color of honey, looked smooth and unlined. He saw a great deal of it, from her hairline to the generous swell of her breasts that were cuddled and lifted by the black satin of her corset, from the graceful curve of her shoulder to the tips of her slender fingers. Her snug, black leather pants and tall, black boots covered everything else, hugging her curves with loving care and making his body tighten.

Lord, she is stunning.

He *felt* stunned. He hadn't reacted to the mere sight of a woman in longer than he could remember, but he reacted to this one. Already he could feel his cock hardening beneath his trousers, filling with blood and heat, while his sense of boredom died a sharp death.

She stood out in stark contrast, relieved against the sea of sameness that surrounded her. She, too, had dressed all in black, but she shared nothing else with the other women in the room. Her skin had the pearlescent glow of natural fairness, and her hair had not been dyed a flat and light absorbing black. It rippled over her shoulders and down her back in waves of burnished mahogany. When she turned her head, the light caught it and sparked dancing flames across the shiny surface. Dmitri imagined burying his hands in it, using his grip to hold her still while he drove into her body.

He wanted that body, he acknowledged, wanted to feel those pale, white curves against him, under him. Her body flowed beneath clinging, black cloth and stiff metal boning in a reflection of Venus's glory. Smooth, graceful shoulders curved down to generous breasts, and the corset accentuated the way her waist nipped in waspishly beneath their enticing fullness. Her hips flared from that narrow span, round and lush and firm, and her legs, gloved by the smooth leather pants, looked round and soft and perfect for clasping around his hips, or throwing over his shoulders, or tangling firmly with his.

He sat there at the bar, staring and fantasizing and wanting her, and while he did so, he gave in to his instincts and slipped lightly inside her mind.

She didn't notice him, as wrapped up in her thoughts as she was, but he'd have been astounded if she had. Most people didn't notice his mental presence even when he didn't keep quiet, like he did now. Very few people out there had any sort of psychic talent, and even fewer knew how to use it. He didn't probe deeply enough into the woman's mind to see if she did; he just wanted to get a sense of her, to decide if more than her beautiful body intrigued him.

More than intrigued, he found himself entranced and unexpectedly entertained. This woman possessed a lively mind and a sharp-edged humor.

Look at that. He heard her voice in his head, husky and feminine and arousing. *Lord Velveteen thinks he's just the shit sitting there with those silly little stick figures fawning all over his poet shirt. Does he have any idea how ridiculous it is for a grown man to have a visible ribcage and lacy shirt cuffs? Oh, wait. That's right. He's a long way from a grown man.*

He watched her raise a bottle to her slick, painted mouth, and his eyes narrowed. He wanted those lips to part around his cock, and the violence of his lust surprised him. This woman had an unsettling effect on him.

And that one, he heard her scoff. *How ridiculous does he look? He's got more mascara on than I do, and he didn't even check for clumps. Is he* crooking his finger *at me? Get real, sonny. I'm not about to answer that insulting little summons with a makeup tip, let alone with what you're after.*

Dmitri's head whipped around, and his gaze locked on the mascaraed Romeo. A quick mental push sent the kid reeling back against the bar and put the fear of God into him — or, at least, the fear of Dmitri.

Where is this guy Ava invited? If I have to wait around this circus much longer, he can kiss his chances for some nookie goodbye. I don't care how badly they think I need this. I refuse to fuck someone who can't even manage to show up on time for it.

Rage turned his vision black for a split second, and he actually felt his fangs lengthen in anticipation of the wounds he would inflict on any man who dared to touch her. He would show these pretenders a real vampire's fury if a single one of them thought to lay a hand on what Dmitri intended to claim for his own. His woman would not fuck any man but him.

His woman.

Dmitri registered the possessive term with surprise and tested the phrase in his mind. In all his considerable lifetime, he'd never felt such an instant proprietary interest in any woman. He'd never been tempted to conquer and claim so quickly. But in this case, he wanted to mark the woman so the entire world would know to keep its distance.

When he saw the woman turn her gaze to him, he ruthlessly tamped down his emotions and moved his touch to the edge of her mind. He didn't think she had noticed his presence within her, but he felt it prudent to be cautious. Already, he detected a stubborn and independent streak in her. He didn't want her to struggle against him. Not yet.

He felt her gaze on him, and he met her stare with a bold one of his own. Heat arced between them, slicing through the crowd as if to remove all barriers separating them. He wanted no barriers, wanted her bared to him, body and mind, so he could sate himself with her flesh, her thoughts and her blood.

She was perfect, and she would be his.

Chapter Three

Lord, but he is scrumptious.

Unable to keep from staring, Reggie decided even if this wasn't Ava's friend, he was the only man she wanted tying her to a bed, thank you very much.

He perched on his barstool with the lazy, elegant grace of a panther, and his thick, dark hair looked as glossy as a panther's furry hide. It capped a face of arresting sensuality. She couldn't call him handsome, not with features so firm and chiseled they looked like they'd been cut from granite, but she could definitely call him yummy. In fact, she'd just adore eating him all up.

His hard features matched his body, or what she could see of it from across the room. He had the graceful, muscled physique of the big cat she'd already compared him to, with broad shoulders, long, muscular legs and a lean, flat stomach. His dark, casual clothes suited him and drew attention to his impressive frame.

She found herself craning her head to see him better through the milling crowd. A knowing smile curved his sensual mouth, and Reggie blushed, cheeks flaming even harder when another gorgeous male specimen stopped beside her mystery man and placed a hand on his shoulder. The newcomer leaned his head down to hear what Mr. Mouthwatering had to say, and when his head turned and his eyes locked on her, she knew they were talking about her.

Oh, my. Apparently the truly drop-dead gorgeous travel in packs, she thought, when she got a good look at Mr. Hunk's friend.

The second man had a body covered in the lean, hard muscle of a runner, and his toffee highlighted, chocolaty dark hair looked like it needed a good cut. His skin was darker than Mr. Oohlala's, but he had the same sort of commanding presence and authoritative stare.

She waited for the same surge of lust that had hit her the moment she saw the first mystery man, but nothing happened. Her brain appreciated the friend made a truly appealing decoration, but she experienced no urge to tear off her clothes and fling her body against his. Shifting her gaze to Mr. Magnificent, she felt her hands reaching toward her zipper.

Across the bar, her mystery man laughed out loud, and she heard the sound even over the din of music and conversation. She felt it, too. It vibrated in the pit of her stomach and aroused her like a caress. Her pussy dampened.

Okay, Reg, get a grip, she instructed herself, breaking eye contact and looking around for her friends. Maybe they could distract her from her hormone attack. Danice still gyrated on the dance floor, this time partnered with a refugee punk with a burgundy mohawk. Corinne had joined them and danced with the guy Danice had left behind. At least Ava and Missy were still with her, and Ava wouldn't budge until her friend got there. She thought she could count on Missy, too, but even as the thought crossed her mind, a group of women stopped next to their table and launched a babbling greeting of pleasure and surprise at seeing Melissa Roper, their old pal from college, here at the nightclub. Grateful for the chance to focus on something other than Mr. TakeMeNow, Reggie pasted on a smile and let Missy introduce her to the other women.

Their small table suddenly became the place to be in the crowded club. The friends seemed to breed more friends, and their numbers swelled from four to seven. Reggie stepped back to make room for yet another one of them to hug Missy hello and found herself maneuvered entirely away from the table. An elbow struck her in the small of her back, and she turned to glare at whoever hadn't watched where he was going. She scanned the crowd, but no one looked close enough to be the culprit. Sighing, she turned back toward Missy and the college friends only to realize she'd lost their table completely. Somehow, when her back was turned, she'd been swept away in the crowd and couldn't even see where Missy and Ava had been standing.

She started to get angry before another thought struck her. If she couldn't see her friends, they couldn't see her. She could make good her escape!

Suddenly, she felt like she'd just managed a prison break. Now she just had to avoid the warden and the bloodhounds long enough to make it through the front door, and she'd be a free woman.

She wasted no time. Ducking behind a tall man in purple latex, she started to weave a path through the bar and toward the front entrance. She'd gotten maybe five feet before a hand closed around her elbow and pulled her to a halt.

"Surely you are not leaving yet, *malishka*?"

Reggie rocked to a halt on her four-inch heels and froze. She felt the warm hand on her skin and the dark presence beside her, but everything else disappeared. Even the throb of the music faded into the background. Reggie refused to acknowledge whether or not anything else had taken up throbbing instead.

The voice that spoke from slightly behind wasn't nearly as surprising as the firm, warm hand that slid down over the smooth satin of her corset to settle with intimate possession on her hip. Her head snapped up, and she found herself looking into the intense, black eyes of the stranger from the end of the bar.

Wow. He's even yummier up close.

That was her initial reaction, followed closely by an embarrassed blush when he smiled down at her with a lazy sort of amusement, as if she'd spoken her comments aloud. *That's impossible, Regina. He's just a guy, not a Psychic Friend. So get a grip. And what is he doing with his hands on me, anyway? I know I've never seen him before. He is not the sort of thing a girl forgets.*

She figured that last thought qualified her for an MU degree—Master of Understatement. The man looked like sin walking. Easily over six feet tall, probably six-two or six-three, his impressive muscles were even more intimidating up close. His thick, dark hair looked black in the dim light and fell in unruly waves over his forehead. He needed a cut, and she might just decide to get a styling license to have an excuse to run her fingers through that hair.

His eyes, so dark they appeared black, laughed down at her, though his luscious, chiseled lips remained firm in his granite-hewn face.

She opened her mouth to speak, but he tightened the hand on her hip just a little, enough to distract her from what she'd been about to say.

"I had hoped you would allow me to buy you a drink," the dark voice rumbled again, and Reggie saw Mr. YumYum had a look of amusement in his black, bedroom eyes. Amusement and something more. Under the glint of humor, his eyes were watchful and intense and blazing with heat. Reggie did not consider herself the type of girl who let strange men pick her up in bars. Still, she had enough sense to regret that while she stared up at him and unthinkingly licked her lips.

The stranger's eyes blazed hotter, and his hand on her stomach shifted to bring her closer. The action managed to snap Reggie out of her daze.

She scrambled to regain her equilibrium — something she'd never had a problem with before Tall, Dark and Sinful had shown up — and turned to face him. "I never let strange men buy me drinks. You never know which one might be the next Jack the Ripper."

His mouth quirked up at one corner. "I promise I have no fondness for dark alleys, nor for prostitutes. But if it would make you feel better, you may buy me a drink instead."

She thought that might prove to be just as dangerous. "Um, I suppose I should thank you for the offer, Mr…whoever you are, but I don't think so."

She attempted to step back, to reinforce her words with some distance — a buffer zone against his enormous sex appeal — but the stranger held on tight and merely smiled at her.

"Dmitri." He murmured, that wickedly amused look she'd noticed earlier back on his face. "My name is Dmitri Vidâme. And you have not, really."

"Not what?"

"Thanked me."

It took a struggle, but Reggie managed to overcome her desire to melt at the sight of his sexy, mischievous smile and forced her eyes to roll instead. "For offering to 'let' me buy you a drink? That's not the sort of offer that inspires me to thank you by inviting you back to my place and showing you my gratitude naked."

Dmitri chuckled, a rough, rumbling sound that rasped over her senses like the tongue of a great big cat. "I had not thought you should. I was merely giving you the opportunity to voice your thanks in the conventional manner. But if you prefer to do this while naked—" His eyebrows shot up, and his grin deepened. "—it would be rude of me to gainsay you, no?"

Reggie blushed. Even though she'd brought up the whole naked thing, somehow the idea sounded a lot more wicked on his lips than it ever had on hers. She cleared her throat and again tried to step back. Again his hand tightened on her belly, but this time it was joined by its mate. Both hands slid over the warm silk of her corset and settled possessively on her hips. He drew her even closer. Reggie looked down to see somehow she'd been led without her notice. Dmitri had backed up until he sat at the bar again, and he pulled her to him until she stood between his spread legs, close enough to smell the earthy, spicy scent of him. She took a deep, involuntary breath, savoring his fragrance, until his chuckle broke the spell, and her eyes snapped open.

She hadn't even realized they were closed.

"Look, Mr. Vidâme, why don't I go back to my friends and you can go back to your friend." She blurted out the suggestion, which just showed her nerves had gotten out of control. This man could easily turn her into a babbling idiot...if it wasn't already too late. "I saw him talking to you earlier—"

"Misha."

"—and I'm sure the two of you had plans for...huh?" She stopped, the gorgeous friend forgotten.

"You will not call me Mr. Vidâme, Regina," he instructed. "You will call me Dmitri, at the very least. Though I would prefer you call me Misha. It is a nickname. A term of endearment."

He said it as if he wanted to become dear to her.

Reggie shook her head to clear out the cobwebs she could feel forming. "Wait. How did you know my name? You couldn't have heard my friends over the music."

"Actually, I have exceptional hearing, but your friends only called you by that horrid nickname. Reggie is a name for a man, not for one as beautiful as you." His eyes roamed over her in frank appreciation. "Nor so obviously a woman."

Reggie blushed at his compliment, which only made her madder. "Don't try and sweet talk me, buster. I've had enough of that kind of crap. In fact, I've had enough of this conversation. Now take your hands off me."

Dmitri raised an eyebrow and lifted his hands from her hips, holding his palms up so she could see they no longer restrained her. "You are always free to go, Regina. If that is truly your wish."

She didn't trust the velvet purr in his voice, nor the amused expression on his face. She took a step backward.

Or, to be precise, she *tried* to take a step backward. She pictured herself taking a step backward. She could practically feel the impulse running down the nerve endings from her brain to her legs, but her feet remained stubbornly motionless. Since she'd already shifted her weight backward in anticipation of that step, she nearly fell on her ass. She teetered for a moment, on the verge of an embarrassing thump, and reached out to steady herself. Instead of catching the cool wood of the bar, her hands caught the solid warmth of Dmitri's thighs, encased in soft, black denim. As soon as she steadied herself, she snatched her hands back as if they burned.

They only tingled.

"What the hell is going on?"

Dmitri shrugged. "I did as you asked, *dushka*. I have taken my hands off you. I have told you that you are free to go." He leaned closer to her until she could feel his breath brush her skin. "You must not want to leave me."

"Bullshit," Reggie said, trying to cover her growing unease. "You've done something to me, and I want to know what the hell it is. No, actually, I don't care what you're doing, I just want you to stop it and let me go."

She braced her hands against his legs and pushed, but her feet remained stubbornly glued to the floor. Dmitri leaned forward, and she turned her head, straining to get away. One large, masculine hand touched her hip and trailed up her side, skirting the outside of her breast until it closed over her chin, gently but firmly turning her back to face him. He forced her eyes to meet his, capturing her gaze and holding it as surely as he held her feet in place. Which she knew he was doing. Somehow.

"Do you really?" he murmured, nuzzling her cheek so his hint of stubble rasped against her skin. His other hand slid around her hip to rest in the small of her back and press her closer. His thighs tightened, and he surrounded her, held her caged and confined and unable to escape. She couldn't even tear her gaze from his. His dark eyes restrained her as securely as his hands drew her deeper, until she wondered if it would be so bad to drown in those glittering, black pools.

Do you really want me to leave you?

Helpless, seduced, she felt her head slowly shake from side to side. *No.*

Dmitri smiled again, but this time the expression appeared dangerous and male and predatory, rather than amused. *I thought not. You want to belong to me, Regina, as much as I want you to be mine.*

His voice rumbled over her, around her, until it was the only thing in her universe, the only thing other than his hands and his skin and his dark, dark eyes. Yet even as he spoke to her, she could see the play of desire and satisfaction on his lips. Lips that never moved.

Reggie froze, her eyes going wide, her lips parting, and her breath grinding to a halt. "Oh, my God," she whispered, still unable to move, but equally unable to believe she had heard this man speaking to her inside her head, had felt him holding her in place even when he ceased to touch her. "Who are you?"

His hand slid from her chin to cup her face, his fingers tangling in the soft silk of her hair. And still his eyes held hers, keeping her still and enthralled. *I have told you, dushka, I am Dmitri Vidâme. And I will be your lover.*

* * * * *

Reggie couldn't remember their last few minutes at the bar, but she remembered the feel of Dmitri's palm on the bare skin between her shoulder blades. She didn't remember saying goodbye to her friends, or paying for her drink, but she remembered his hands on her waist while he walked behind her and guided her through the crowd to the front door.

She didn't remember the cab ride home, but she remembered the steely strength of Dmitri's thighs beneath her as she sat on his lap and rested her head on his firm shoulder. She remembered his fingers cupping her breasts through the heavy silk of her corset, his thumbs making teasing swipes over her tight nipples. She remembered one of those incredible hands drifting over her stomach and cupping possessively over her pussy, making the flesh tingle and throb beneath her leather pants, but she didn't remember leaving the cab and entering her apartment building.

Her memory neglected to store the ride in the elevator up to her floor, or the long walk down the empty corridor to her apartment, but she would never forget the silent, overwhelming presence of the man who walked beside her.

She couldn't recall unlocking her door, but she remembered the feel of Dmitri's body, the heat of him when he crowded close behind her, urging her into the dark room and closing the door behind them.

She remembered nothing until he flipped the switch on her bedside lamp and her consciousness turned on as well. She came back to herself in a flash and found herself standing in the middle of her bedroom with her nipples hard and her pussy aching and the hot, dark depths of his eyes threatening to swallow her whole.

"Oh my god," she said, taking a frightened step back. A surge of adrenaline made her tremble, and she locked her knees to keep from falling. "What are you doing to me?"

"Only as you wish, *dushka*," he murmured, prowling toward her in the dim light. "Only what pleases you."

She retreated from him, shaking her head. "You can't be real. *This* can't be real. I must have made you up, because no one could possibly do what you're doing to me."

"What am I doing to you, Regina?"

Making me want to beg for your touch.

She ignored her thought. "You're scaring me." It sounded like a much safer response.

He moved closer, and she retreated. They danced those same steps until he backed her into the smooth wood of her bedroom door, and Reggie had nowhere else to go.

He leaned close. "It is not fear that causes your heart to race, *milaya*." He reached out, and she jerked back from his touch, but he just brushed a stray tendril of hair from her face and held her gaze with his. "It is not fear that makes your breath quick and your mouth dry. It is not fear that tightens your nipples and dampens your cunt. It is want."

Reggie's thighs clenched. His words made her hotter than she'd been the last time she'd come, and he wasn't even touching her.

"You can't be doing this to me," she said, hoping she could make the words true by speaking them. "This can't happen."

Dmitri chuckled, a deep, rumbling sound that resonated in her head and her heart and deep inside her pussy.

"You will be amazed by all the things that can happen, *milaya*, if you will just let go and trust me."

She wanted it so badly she scared herself, and a frightened Reggie was a belligerent Reggie.

"Trust you?" she scoffed, stiffening her spine and glaring up at him. "I don't even know you! I just picked you up in a bar. You could be anyone. Or any *thing*. How am I supposed to trust you?"

She braced herself for his anger and almost hoped for it. If he were angry, maybe she wouldn't want so badly to rip off all her clothes and jump him.

She was glad she could still speak her mind, though. It comforted her to know no matter what this weird power he had over her, he hadn't turned her into some mindless sex drone. As long as she could still recognize herself, her fear stopped short of panic and terror.

Dmitri smiled, not an angry roar in sight. "You make excuses for yourself, Regina. Yet even as you do so, you know in your heart that the point is moot. Part of you already trusts me, or I would not be here. You would not have invited me into your home. Into your bed."

She resented the way his voice could make her ache for him. "I invited you into my bed, huh? Is that what I've done? It's funny, because I don't seem to recall saying that little thing."

"You do not have to speak for me to know your desires, *dushka*. I know precisely what you want, for it is what I want as well."

Knowing you want to tie me down and fuck me 'til my brain explodes is hardly comforting, buster.

Tamping down her wayward thoughts, she opened her eyes wide and batted her lashes up at him. "Really? You want an end to world hunger and a 1968 Jaguar sedan in British Racing Green?"

"You should be careful not to sass me too much, Regina Elaina." All at once, the three inches between their bodies became no inches, and he cupped his hands around her ass, kneading the flesh through the form-fitting leather. "I may have to punish you."

Yes, please!

Reggie cursed herself and the juices that seeped from her pussy at the thought of it. Instead of the fear, his statement aroused nothing but her nipples and her curiosity. And her pussy. Couldn't forget her pussy. No matter how hard she tried.

Her lips parted before she could stop them, and she was left to listen in horror when her tongue ran wild and teased the tiger.

"Oh, really?" She barely recognized her own voice for all the seductive purring. "And would you like to punish me, Dmitri?"

His eyes glinted, and his hands squeezed her ass. "As much as you would like to be punished, *katyonak*."

"What does it mean?" And could he please give her a lengthy explanation so she'd have time to think of an escape route?

"*Katyonak?*"

"Yes."

"It is an endearment. It means 'kitten.'"

Something in Reggie melted, and this time it wasn't even her cunt. "Is that how you think of me? An innocent little kitten?"

He raised one hand to cup her face, lowered the other until his fingers slid between her ass cheeks and pressed against her leather-covered core from behind.

"An adventurous little kitten," he corrected, flicking one finger over the smooth, hot leather, "bent on mischief. Soft and sensuous and filled with curiosity, but still just a bit skittish."

With one hand on her face and his other hand cupping her pussy through her increasingly uncomfortable leather pants, Reggie felt bound more tightly than iron shackles could have managed. This man had complete control over her body, and the look in his eyes told her he wanted it that way.

She trembled.

"Am I right, *katyonak*? Do I make you nervous?"

She trembled again, and her body shivered against his, bringing a very wicked smile to his lips. His hand pressed harder against her, and her labia spread for him, parting around the seam in the crotch of her pants. Suddenly even the thick leather seemed like no barrier at all.

He had the advantage, and he pressed it. The hand he hadn't already buried between her legs slid down from her jaw to close around her throat, not squeezing, but circling it like a collar and pressing her head gently back against the door. The position forced her spine to straighten even further than the corset alone had managed, and she stood there, pinned between his hard body and the hard wood, unable to look at anything but him.

He stared into her eyes, his thumb smoothing the skin of her vulnerable throat while his other hand began to rub the furrow between her thighs with firm, steady pressure. She felt like a toy, positioned for his pleasure, dominated and controlled beneath his hands and his eyes and his breathtaking presence.

So why the hell was she so excited?

Why did she have to fight to keep from whimpering, to keep her eyes from drifting shut, to keep her thighs from parting wider to urge him closer. Should she really enjoy being treated like some sort of blow up doll for a strange man to use?

"You have nothing in common with such inanimate objects, *milka*. A doll does not enjoy her lover's caress." His fingers slid forward between her puffy lips, pressing the rough seam against her tender flesh, until he nudged her clit. Reggie bit back a moan but couldn't control the way her hips rolled into his touch. "Only a woman becomes so hot, so wet, so richly scented."

He inhaled deeply, breathing her in. Reggie saw the way his nostrils flared and the heat that burned in his eyes and wondered how she smelled to him.

Then she wondered what the hell she was thinking. She tensed, and nerves overwhelmed her again, no matter how wet her pussy got.

"That is very good, Regina," he murmured, nuzzling the sensitive hollow behind her ear. He might as well have nuzzled her clit, because his touch made her gasp and shake. "I want to make you nervous. And I want to make you wet. Before the night is over, I want to make you do many, many things you've only imagined. And that is what you want as well."

She wanted to deny it, wanted to tell him he bored her and he should leave her alone. But his fingers slid forward and closed over her clit. When he squeezed, she came.

Her body tensed and shuddered against the cold, wooden door. Her hips jerked hard against his hand, and her pussy slicked the crotch of her leather pants with her juices. She stood there, dazed and breathless, held up not by her water-weak legs, but by his hand on her throat and his fingers on her spasming cunt.

"Isn't that what you want, Regina?"

She thought about denying it. She *longed* to deny it, but she knew he could feel the way her pussy still fluttered beneath its covering. She couldn't lie, but she didn't want to admit it either so she kept her mouth shut and glared at him instead.

He smiled and twisted his hand until his knuckles dug into the soaking leather on either side of her sensitized clit. He flexed his fingers, and she whimpered.

"Isn't it?"

"God, yes!"

"Good girl."

All of a sudden his hands fell away from her, and she sagged boneless against the door. "What—?"

She hadn't had time to blink, but Dmitri stood several feet away, his lips curved in a hard, wicked smile. He looked so pleased with himself. If her pussy weren't still throbbing, she'd be tempted to wipe the smirk off his face.

"Patience, *dushka*," he murmured, looking amused by her mutinous expression. "You shall have what you want."

His eyes gleamed, and she could have sworn she felt his hands on her again, rubbing slowly over her swollen breasts and simultaneously cupping her dripping pussy, circling her wrists and kneading her ass. If he hadn't been standing three feet away, she would have been tempted to believe he'd grown a hundred new hands. She could feel his touch everywhere. *Sensory memory*, she told herself. Never mind that he hadn't held her by her wrists.

"You shall have exactly what you crave, Regina, but only if you do as I say. Can you do that?"

She hesitated, wanting to say no, to scream, to run for the hills. At least, that's what her mind wanted to do. Her pussy wanted to wrap around his cock and milk him until they were both raw. She wasn't inclined to give her pussy the deciding vote.

But then her nipples chimed in, followed by her thighs, her arms, her ass and, finally, her traitorous lips.

"Yes. I can do that."

She thought she caught a warm flash of pride and pleasure before his expression firmed into a mask of impassive control.

"Good girl. In that case, strip off the leather and get on the bed. But leave the corset where it is."

Chapter Four

It took a minute for the command to sink in, but once it did, Reggie swallowed. Hard.

Strip? Now? Here?

"Strip," he repeated. "Now. Here."

He leaned against the post at the foot of her bed and watched.

She bit her lip. Moment of truth time. Her body wanted the clothes off her back and Dmitri on her front. Her mind called her ten kinds of idiot. Her curiosity cast the deciding vote. When would she ever have this kind of opportunity again, especially with a man who made her this hot? She couldn't back out now.

Her hands moved to the side zipper on her leather pants, but her eyes stayed on his face. Just looking at his firm, authoritative expression and his austere, compelling face sent a shiver down her spine. She couldn't read his thoughts, but her body didn't care. Her nipples tightened beneath their silk covering, and she slowly lowered the zipper.

"You might want to take the boots off first," he drawled, watching but not moving. "Unless you want to be stuck with your pants around your ankles and no place to go. Not that the image doesn't have a certain naughty schoolgirl appeal." His eyes glinted, the only crack in his stoic demeanor. "But we'll save that particular scene for another time. Boots first."

The images sprang into her mind like an ambush. She saw herself, bare-bottomed and draped over his knees to face the consequences of her disobedience. He would be stern and unyielding, and she would be shaking and repentant, with an ass that glowed pink and warm from her spanking. A shudder raced through her.

Dmitri noticed. His eyes burned, and she felt the force of his satisfaction.

Her cheeks flushed even hotter, and she hurried to obey him. She reached down to pull off her boots and realized she had a problem.

She bent to a thirty-five degree angle before the confining corset jerked her to a halt. She was stuck, and all of a sudden she recalled a key detail of her wardrobe, like the fact that she'd put on the corset after the boots; and they could only come off in the opposite order.

She straightened up and cleared her throat. "Um, I seem to have a small problem."

Dmitri quirked an eyebrow.

"I can't untie the boots while I'm wearing the corset."

He said nothing.

Reggie suspected he knew exactly what her problem was, but she explained anyway. "I can't bend over far enough. Unless I take off the corset."

At least that got him to speak.

"Did I tell you to take off the corset?" he asked with the exaggerated patience of an adult to a slow-witted child.

He made Reggie feel like that naughty schoolgirl, and she quickly blocked out that thought before it got her in any more trouble. She shrugged. "You said to leave the corset where it is."

"Precisely."

She shifted her weight and frowned. "But I told you I can't take the boots off while the corset is on. And I can't take the pants off until the boots come off."

He just raised his other eyebrow, and Reggie snapped.

"Fine then!" She crossed her arms over her chest and glared at him. "If I can't take the boots off, you have to find some other way to get into my pants, buster."

Reggie savored her defiance for all of three milliseconds. Until she saw Dmitri's eyes narrow. His jaw firmed, and he pushed away from the bedpost, taking one menacing step toward her.

"I don't believe I heard you properly, Regina," he purred. This time the rasp sounded more like a threat than a rumble of pleasure. "Did you just talk back to me? Because if you did, I'm afraid you'll have to be punished for it."

For a heartbeat, she contemplated sassing him again. Not only would it give her great emotional satisfaction, but it would be the tug on the tiger's tale that likely *would* get her turned over his knee and spanked until she begged for mercy. And if she egged him into it, she wouldn't have to take responsibility for it. She could blame him.

She quivered. Dmitri stepped in front of her until his chest pressed against her and his breath tickled her eyelashes. He clouded her mind with the feel of him. Her stomach did a back flip, and suddenly, defying him was the last thing on her mind. She wanted to please him, needed to win his approval and his touch.

"I'm sorry," she whispered.

He gripped her chin in his hand, raising her eyes to meet his. "What did you say, Regina? I couldn't hear you."

She licked her lips, fought back another shudder. Every time she drew breath, she smelled him, and the earthy, spicy scent of him made her pussy clench. "I said I was sorry. I didn't mean to…to talk back to you like that."

Dmitri watched her, staring at her as if he measured her words and her sincerity and weighed them against her offense. His thumb stroked the tender underside of her jaw until her breath caught in her throat. He smiled.

"Better," he murmured, "but still not a proper apology. Who are you apologizing to? Me? Your bedroom? The universe?"

She chewed on her lip and frowned. "To you."

"And so you should, but I could not tell that from your apology. When you tell someone you are sorry, you should address him properly."

The look in his eyes told her he wanted something, even though she didn't know what. The feel of his hands on her, especially when the other slid to the small of her back and pressed her hips firmly against the ridge of his erection, made her want to squirm. Her pussy ached and dripped, and her nipples hurt from beading so tightly. She needed relief, and she wondered what she would have to do to get it.

A thought occurred to her.

"Do you want me to—" She broke off and blushed. "I mean, should…should I…should I call you…Master?"

What was the proper etiquette for this kind of situation? Emily Post needed to add a chapter.

His mouth curved in a slow, hot smile, and his hand slid from her chin to the nape of her neck. His fingers tangled in her hair and began to massage the hollow at the base of her skull. The feeling traveled down her spine until her thighs clenched.

"I have already told you what I wish you to call me," he whispered. "Do you not remember?"

She nodded slowly and moistened her dry lips. "Misha."

"Yes. You will call me Misha, Regina, for you will not need so obvious a reminder of what I am to you."

Which meant he would be her master. Part of her rebelled, but other, more demanding parts rejoiced.

He leaned forward and pressed a soft kiss to her forehead. Then he released her and resumed his position at the foot of her bed. "Now, I believe I told you to remove your boots."

Boots? What boots? Oh, yeah. The man could put her in a daze faster than a two-by-four to the forebrain. She shook her head and reached for her feet. And found herself right back where she had started. She might be short, but in the confining corset, her boots were still a long way out of her reach.

She straightened up and cleared her throat. "I'm sorry, Misha, but I can't reach my boots to unlace them." She worried her bottom lip between her teeth, and then took the plunge. "Would you please help me take them off?"

She saw his approval and felt absurdly proud of herself.

"Since you asked so nicely, *dushka*, I would be happy to help you." He beckoned her to him. "Come and put your foot up on the bedrail where I can reach it. You can still bend from the hips."

She obeyed, crossing to the bed and raising her left foot to the rail beside his thigh. The position spread her legs, showcasing her pussy beneath the damp leather, and she caught a hint of her own fragrance. She saw Dmitri inhale deeply, and she quivered.

He pushed her cuff high enough to unlace her calf-length boots. His hands moved with brisk efficiency, and she couldn't wait to feel them on her again. Her heart skipped a beat when the thought finally sank in that once he removed her boots and she dropped her pants, she would be able to feel his touch on her exposed pussy. Just the thought almost sent her back over the edge.

She needed a quick distraction. "What does that word mean? The one you keep calling me."

He pulled her laces free and tapped her right thigh. She obediently switched legs, lowering the left and propping the right on the bedrail.

"*Dushka* means 'sweet' or 'sweetie.' *Milaya* and *milka* mean 'sweet little girl.'" He finished with her second boot and pushed it to the floor. His eyes met hers. "I have not yet tasted you, Regina, but already I know you will be very sweet on my tongue."

Oh, Lord. Her eyes all but rolled back in her head. The man talked a good game.

He grinned. "Now get back where you were and do as you were told. And this time, no backtalk."

Reggie took a deep breath and nodded. Her knees wobbled like rubber, so she stepped carefully back into position. She was putting on a show for him, but the idea excited rather than offended her. She wanted him to be aroused by the sight of her. She wanted her body to incite his lust. She wanted to trip him and beat him to the floor.

She toed her boots off, trying not to imagine the feel of his tongue against her overheated flesh. If her imagination didn't cut it out, she wouldn't even last until he got around to fucking her. She'd burst into flame the moment he laid a hand on her.

Even his gaze threatened to singe her. She felt it like a wave of heat traveling up the length of her legs and coming to rest at the curve of her hip, right at her zipper. Quickly, she slid the metal tab down and hooked her thumbs in the waistband of her pants. She started to push the heavy material down, but a burst of nerves stopped her. She couldn't believe she was really doing this, stripping herself naked for a man she'd just met. Maybe she should just—

He growled.

He didn't speak, didn't tsk his tongue, didn't clear his throat. He growled like a predator, and she thought his lips curved in something just short of a snarl.

Maybe she should just take off her pants.

Squelching the nerves and the temptation to turn tail and run—mostly because she figured he'd just chase her—she slid the leather over her hips and down her thighs as far as she could without bending over. Stepping out of the confining material with as much grace as she could muster, she kicked it aside and found herself all but naked in front of him.

Unable to postpone it any longer, she lifted her gaze to his.

If black could burn, his eyes burned in that moment. His gaze started at her toes and slid up along the length of her bare legs, tickling her skin like a caress. The heat made her shiver, and she imagined how her nerves would riot when he finally touched her.

She watched his eyes, wanted his hands, but when his gaze reached the vee of her legs and the flare of her hip, it cooled and made her shiver.

"Take off the panties," he ordered, his voice rougher than before. Deeper. "And don't wear them again. They get in my way, and I want you always available to me. Do you understand?"

She nodded. She could hardly deny it when his words sent a rush of moisture flooding from her pussy. She ignored the pounding of her heart and stripped off the damp, green thong. "Yes, Misha."

"Good. Now get on the bed. This is the second time I've had to tell you."

And don't make me tell you again.

His voice had been neutral, but Reggie caught the subtext. He wanted obedience. The weird thing was she wanted to give it.

Swift and a little jerky with nerves, she crossed the few steps to the bed and crawled onto the velvety chenille spread. She knelt there, perched awkwardly on her heels, unsure of what to do next. Her hands fluttered, wanting to cover her naked pubis, wanting to touch him. In the end, she forced them to her sides.

Dmitri watched from the foot of the bed, his dark eyes glowing in the dim light, his expression bland. He was driving her crazy. His nonchalance had built the tension inside her to a breaking point. With every breath her nipples ached and her pussy throbbed and her palms itched with the need to feel him against her.

She wanted him to talk to her, to touch her, to take her. He needed to do something before she lost her mind, even if that thing meant throwing her down and fucking her senseless without an iota of foreplay. For God's sake, the entire night with him had been foreplay. She wanted *now*play.

He stepped around to the side of the bed and stood in front of her. "Face me," he ordered, "and open your legs."

She bit her lip and obeyed, but there was no way she could meet his gaze while she did. She looked down instead, but her vision became filled with the sight of her own pale thighs and the dark valley between them. Her pussy leaked like a faucet, and she could see little drops of her juices beaded in the close-cropped curls between her legs.

"Wider."

Trembling, her breath coming faster, she obeyed, shifting her weight to maintain her balance while she spread herself open before him.

He extended his hand and laid one long finger against the skin at the inside of her knee. While she watched, he drew it slowly up the inside of her thigh until his fingers tangled in her damp curls. He rubbed, and she stopped breathing.

One finger tapped firmly against her inner thigh.

"Wider."

She opened wider, spreading inch by inch until he finally stopped tapping. She could have pressed the soles of her feet together, and the muscles in her groin and thighs trembled to hold the position.

God, she felt so exposed. Her shiver had nothing to do with cold.

She couldn't meet his gaze, couldn't look away from the sight of her own body, spread lewdly wide and naked for his pleasure. She felt the cool air against her hot flesh, saw the deep red of her labia and the dark, fiery brown of her curls.

And she saw his hand, large and strong and possessive upon her.

"Very nice," he murmured while his fingertips twirled and tangled in her curls. "I am pleased to see you know how to behave yourself, *dushka*."

His fingers flexed, pulling the short strands of hair and tugging little pinpricks of pain from her skin. The sweet, sharp sensations made her pussy clench and forced a moan from her throat.

Her eyes drifted shut until his free hand raised her chin and he ordered her to look at him.

"You look very pretty like this, Regina." His hand left her chin and smoothed over her until skin faded to silk and his palm rested in the valley of her tightly corseted waist. "But do you know why a woman in a corset is really so appealing to a man?"

His voice sounded casual, even indifferent, but the feel of his lean fingers petting her mound made Reggie quiver. She couldn't concentrate. She could barely remember the question, but he clearly waited for an answer.

"Because—" It came out as a squeak, and she cleared her throat to start again. "Because it exaggerates her figure?"

Her hips rocked forward, trying to force his fingers lower. They were so close to her clit, but she didn't want them *close*. She wanted them *on*.

He evaded her.

"Not really," he murmured. "Yes, the corset enhances her figure, but no more than a good bra and a tight pair of jeans. No, there are other reasons. Deeper reasons."

Reggie bit back a moan. The only deeper she cared about in that moment was the deeper caress of his fingers. If he expected her to be able to follow his conversation when his fingertips rested less than two inches from her swollen and needy clit, he was insane.

His fingers began to wander, bypassing her clit and sinking down the curve of her pubis to brush delicately over her slick, flushed lips, and she knew she was insane. The man was driving her crazy. She sucked in her breath with a hiss and canted her hips higher. He only lightened his touch.

"A man sees two irresistible things in a corseted woman." His fingers teased her sensitive tissues while his tone sounded like a professor at the lectern. She wanted to kill him.

Right after she tossed him down and raped him.

"First, the restriction on her movement makes it impossible to run from him," he continued, seemingly oblivious to her violent thoughts. "It places her at his mercy, appeals to his primitive instincts. It makes him feel powerful in comparison."

How Dmitri could not feel powerful when his tormenting fingers decided whether she would live or die, Reggie couldn't understand. If he gained more control over her, he would have to force the breath in and out of her lungs. The man was killing her.

A split second later, his hand shifted, and Reggie knew she'd been right. He killed her. His exploring fingers halted and withdrew. She whimpered a protest, but her whimper became a scream when his finger returned, parting her wet folds and plunging deep inside her aching pussy.

Dmitri was a large man with large hands, and the extent of her arousal combined with the swelling of her inner tissue to make that one finger feel as large as a cock. Her pussy felt stretched and full.

"And second…"

He's still talking. How the hell can he talk? Oh, God!

His free hand slid around to her ass, pushing her hips forward and rocking her pelvis against his hand. Her clit bumped his wrist, and she gasped.

Her breathing grew harsh, and he leaned forward, speaking into her ear until she felt his words as much as heard them.

"Second, it reminds him that a woman's body is at its most beautiful when it is bound and shaped by his hands."

She couldn't help herself. She shuddered, her entire body wracked by it, and her pussy flooded Dmitri's hand with moisture. She came on a long, high whimper, her body clenching around his invading finger. She couldn't believe it—one finger and she came like a porn star. What would happen when he actually took off his clothes and got around to fucking her?

Her hands released their death grip on the bedspread and reached up to touch his broad, muscular chest.

"Please, Misha," she whispered. "Won't you take your clothes off? I want to see you. I want to touch you."

"Maybe later, if you continue to be a good girl," he dismissed, removing her hands and placing them flat against the bed beside her hips. "For now, we will continue as I wish. Stay still, and close your eyes."

She closed her eyes and tried not to move, but when his hand slid from between her legs and he stepped away, she whimpered and reached for him. She felt bereft without his touch and his overwhelming presence beside her. The air felt empty where he had stood.

"Hush, *dushka*."

Easy for him to say.

She drew in shallow, shaky breaths and listened hard. She wanted to know what he was doing. Her mind swam with the possibilities, but he moved silently, giving her no clues.

He seemed gone for hours while she knelt there on the bed, panting and exposed like some lewd offering to a pagan god.

Her nerves tingled, but before she could register awareness of his return, he slipped his hand into her hair and tugged, tumbling her back onto the mattress in a blur of silk and skin. Her arms were dragged above her head, wrapped with a soft, silky cord and bound to something solid and immoveable. A second later, his weight shifted, and she felt her thighs pulled apart, her ankles roped with the same type of cord and tied securely to the bedposts.

He accomplished it all so quickly she didn't have time to gasp a protest before she found herself secured spread-eagle to her bed. She just lay there, her head spinning, until the rasp of a zipper knocked her straight back into reality.

Her eyes flew open. "What was that?"

Dmitri chuckled. "Clearly not what you thought," he teased, holding up a half open duffle bag so she could see it. He cast a pointed look to the button fly of his jeans. "Though even if it had been, would that have been a reason for disobeying my commands?"

Her eyes snapped closed, and she shook her head. "No, Misha."

"I thought not." His fingertip brushed the crescent of her lowered eyelashes. "You must try harder if you wish to be a good girl, *milaya*."

She heard him rummaging though the bag and stiffened when she realized he hadn't brought it with him. Her stomach turned a slow somersault when she remembered the bag of tricks her friends had left at her apartment. Her bossy, interfering friends.

Oh, God.

She gave a surreptitious tug at her bindings, but they held fast. The cord Dmitri had used might feel soft against her skin, but it held fast like his knots. Clearly, the man knew what he was doing.

Reggie couldn't decide if his talent for this kind of game meant she should start screaming and hope for nosy neighbors, or bend her knees, wiggle her ass and shout, "Fuck me, big boy!"

In the end, she just lay still and listened to her heart pound. And tried to ignore the images crashing through her mind. Images of herself, bound and helpless while this dark, mysterious stranger positioned her and fucked her and slowly drove her out of her mind.

After endless, agonizing minutes, she caught the muffled thump of the bag against the hardwood floor and felt the dip of the mattress when he moved onto the bed beside her.

"You can open your eyes now."

Reggie did, and wasted no time in scanning the bed and nightstand for whatever implements of destruction he had removed from the duffle. From her limited perspective—the bindings prevented her from lifting anything more than her head—she couldn't see a thing. Wary, she turned back to Dmitri. He looked amused.

"If I wanted you to see what I was doing, I wouldn't have made you close your eyes, would I?" His mouth curved in a little smile, and he ran his fingers across her collarbone, skimming them down her side until they curled around her thigh in a brief, disarmingly affectionate squeeze. "Now I want you to see what I'm doing."

She saw.

She saw those beautiful, powerful hands of his reach up to the bodice of her corset. She saw them shift the heavy layers of silk away from her breast, exposing the hard little nipple. It tightened further in the cool air, and she flinched when the backs of his fingers brushed against it while he folded the fabric under itself and tucked it out of the way. He repeated the action on the other side, making her nipples ache and her breath catch. When he finished, the corset supported her lush breasts, holding them high and full above her, completely exposed to his eyes and his hands.

She saw them offered up to him, pale and swollen and pouting for his touch, but when his thumb and forefinger closed over one erect peak, she stopped seeing. All she could do was feel.

Dmitri pinched, his touch firm, but gentle. Reggie sighed and shifted restlessly. Against her aroused bud, the pressure felt like a caress. She needed more. Her eyes began to drift shut.

"No," he growled. "Look at me."

She struggled to obey.

"You liked that."

He seemed to wait for an answer, so she forced herself to nod.

"But it wasn't enough for you."

God, did he have to point out what a pervert she was? She blushed, but shook her head.

"Then I should not repeat it." He withdrew his hand, and her heart sank.

"No, please," she gasped, arching her back to offer her breasts up to him. "Please, Misha. More."

She felt his silence, counted his pause in her racing heartbeats. His hand slid back to her nipple, and he repeated the pinch with the exact same amount of pressure. "Like that?"

"No," she moaned, shaking her head. "I want...more. Please, Misha." Her voice dropped to a whisper. "Please. Harder."

He removed his hand altogether. "I don't think so. If you cannot be clear with me, I must assume you do not really want this."

The loss of his touch made her chest tighten in fear. "Please don't leave me like this," she whispered, on the verge of tears. "Please, Misha."

"Please, what?" his tone sounded polite, but bored, and she knew he wouldn't cut her any slack.

She wanted to slap his face and walk away, but tied to her own bed, neither was an option. Besides, she wanted him inside her so desperately she was prepared to negotiate.

Hell, she was prepared to surrender.

She licked her dry lips, took a deep breath. "Misha, would you please pinch my nipples harder?"

She heard his silence, felt him stretch it out for long minutes. He knew he tortured her, and she knew he did it on purpose.

"I don't think so," he said abruptly. "I think we need to remind you of your position."

Embarrassment and anger opened Reggie's eyes, and she jerked hard against her bindings, scowling furiously up at him. "What? Somehow being tied half-naked to my bed isn't a good enough reminder?"

She knew she sounded snippy, but damn it, he'd made her beg and he'd refused her. It almost killed her mood.

"Clearly not." He turned his back and reached down to the duffle he'd left on the floor. You must not take those very seriously, or you wouldn't still be talking back to me, would you?" He shook his head and clucked his tongue in admonishment. "No, I think before we go any further, you need a crash course in remembering both your place and your manners."

Her scowl didn't budge, not until he straightened up and turned to face her. At that point, her expression slid right into something less like defiance and more like shock. Bordering on panic.

In his left hand, Dmitri held an impressively sized dildo. In his right, he grasped a black, leather flogger with tails as long as his forearm. Above them both, his expression remained polite and impassive.

"Now then, I think we're ready to get started."

Chapter Five

"Misha? Maybe we could talk about this first..."

He stepped close to the side of the bed until he looked directly down at her. "What do we need to talk about, Regina?"

Damn it. His use of her name failed to reassure her. What had happened to the endearments? She scrambled to regroup. "I just thought...well, this isn't...quite what I was expecting...when I pictured this moment."

"On the contrary," he corrected her, "this is precisely what you were expecting. This is how you envisioned submitting to a man, is it not?"

Reggie frowned. He spoke as if he knew that for sure, as if he read her mind again. And here she'd been doing so well pretending that hadn't happened.

God, what are you thinking? It couldn't *have happened. Things like that just don't happen! This is not an episode of the* X-Files.

"No, it isn't," she protested, ignoring her protesting conscience. A situation like this called for judicious lying. Perhaps even through her teeth. "I thought it would be —"

"Exactly as I have presented it to you," he finished firmly, cutting straight through her excuses. He set the toys down on the nightstand and sat beside her, cupping her cheek in one hand. "Do not lie to me, *dushka*. Not about anything. I will not tolerate it."

"How do you know I'm lying?" She didn't really want an answer, but she didn't want to head back to the scary territory they'd just left, either.

"I know your thoughts, *milaya*. You have a very strong mind. Oh, do not be missish or act as if this shocks you," he said when she tried to look disbelieving. "You knew this at the bar, and yet you still let me bring you home. You feel as drawn to me as I feel to you."

Right. Like she would admit to that one. The last thing this man needed was more ammunition against her. He already had her so hot, she felt like her pussy was melting.

"I'll admit I noticed something weird before now, and I can't deny I'm attracted to you, since I did let you get me naked and tie me up," she conceded. "But I still don't know how you can claim to read my mind. That kind of thing is impossible."

"It is quite possible, as you well know." He sounded impatient. "Shall I prove to you how possible it truly is, Regina Elaina?"

Oh shit. No one ever added her middle name unless she was in really big trouble.

Reggie backpedaled hastily, which was quite a trick, considering her feet were still tied to the bedposts.

"That's not necessary. I'm sure—" She broke off when she saw his expression.

He stared at her, his eyes narrowed, his lips firmed into a thin line.

She braced herself for a wave of anger. Somehow she had the feeling Dmitri's temper could be explosive, but nothing detonated. Instead, she found herself fascinated by the changing expressions that played across his face.

When stern discipline shifted to hunger, followed by amused satisfaction, she decided anger might be a better choice.

"Oh, Regina, you naughty girl," he purred, leaning close and bracing his arms on either side of her. He lowered his face until his breath tickled her skin. "Don't you know it's dangerous to taunt a hungry man?"

She swallowed hard, her eyes wide and wary while she stared into his eyes, only inches from hers. He couldn't possibly know what she imagined.

"I will never let another touch you, *milaya*, but I can give you what you dream of. Would you like me to fulfill your darkest fantasies, Regina?"

She started to shake her head, but when the first touch rasped against her skin, she froze. Her eyes opened impossibly wide, and her lips parted on a soundless gasp. She could see his arms had not moved. His hands remained planted on the mattress on either side of her head, supporting his weight as he leaned over her, yet she felt a dozen hot, eager hands caressing her naked flesh.

Firm fingers tightened around her puckered nipples, pinching and tugging the rosy flesh. Hands slid up her thighs, over the round warmth of her belly. More hands invaded her cunt, pressing and circling her clit, parting her slick labia and penetrating her. She felt one finger enter her, then two, then three, stretching her uncomfortably wide while her lover remained unmoving above her.

The phantom hands multiplied, touching every inch of her skin at once. They kneaded her ass, stroked and probed along the secret cleft, parted her round cheeks and rubbed erotic circles around her rosebud.

Unseen fingers pumped steadily into her dripping pussy, and Reggie cried out. She felt like a dozen lovers caressed her, each demanding a response from her overwhelmed senses. But the only lover she could see remained hard and motionless above her, his black eyes blazing while he watched her shiver on the brink of orgasm.

Fear welled up in her. She couldn't understand what he was doing to her, how he could make her feel these things, and all at once she wanted nothing more than to get away from him and from the power he wielded over her.

"No!" she shouted, trying to twist away from the invisible hands, but they were everywhere, and the silk ropes held her pinned for their exploration.

She squeezed her eyes shut. *They're not real!* She told herself, desperately willing her senses to ignore what her mind couldn't accept. *It's a trick. No one is touching you. No one is here but Dmitri. It's a trick. Ignore it, and it will stop.*

But it didn't stop. The fingers inside her thrust faster, the thumb on her clit rubbed harder, tighter circles, and she began to cry.

"Stop," she whimpered. "Please stop."

The hands froze, not withdrawing, but going completely still. Dmitri's breath stirred the hair beside her ear, but all she could hear was the throbbing beat of her own heart and the ragged sound of her breath sawing in and out of her lungs.

She heard his voice rumbling so close to her ear his lips brushed the sensitive lobe.

"Why should I stop?" he asked, soft and low and purring. "This is what you imagine, late at night, when you stroke your own needy flesh. This is what you feel in your mind when you rub your little clit and fuck yourself with your own little fingers. Why not let me give you what you want, Regina?"

"Because you scare me!" she shouted at him, not caring he could have heard her if she'd only breathed the words. He was that close, but she was crying, and her own fear made her angry.

She opened her eyes and turned her head to glare at him, ignoring the tears that clumped her lashes and blurred her vision.

"Do you want to hear me say it, Misha?" she demanded. "Fine, I'll say it. I'm chickening out. I'm a wimp, a wuss, a coward, who never should have gotten myself into this situation to begin with. I'm terrified! Is that what you want to hear? I'm not ready. I can't handle this. Clearly I'm not ready to give in to someone else's control, no matter how sexy I find you."

She sniffled, hating that she couldn't wipe away her tears, that he could see her crying and vulnerable. He still didn't move.

"Now, if you'll just untie me, I'll go make an appointment with a shrink and you can get the hell out of my apartment. Happy?"

"I am becoming much more so." Dmitri answered her rant and her glare with a smile and a tender kiss on the tip of her nose. He sat up, and the phantom hands disappeared. "I told you I wanted you to be completely honest with me, Regina. That includes telling me about your desires and your fears in equal measure."

"You never said that. You told me not to lie. You never mentioned complete honesty."

"Then clearly I should have. I do want your complete honesty, *dushka*, with yourself as well as with me. It is not shameful to fantasize about things you do not actually desire to have, but I will not tolerate it if you lie to me. Do you understand?"

Reggie nodded and shifted restlessly. He still hadn't made a move to free her.

"Well, what are you waiting for?" she demanded. "Now that I've spoiled all your fun, aren't you going to untie me and get going?"

For the first time, Reggie heard him laugh. It sounded rich and dark and utterly sinful, like good chocolate.

Did I just compare his laugh to a food product? After he invaded my mind and made me cry? God, I really do need that shrink…

"You spoiled nothing for me, *milka*. And I didn't say I am finished with you yet."

Her eyes widened. "Uh, wait a second, buddy. In this country, when we say, 'Stop now and untie me,' the implied subtext there is, 'Or I will call the police and see your sorry ass rot in jail for rape.' Maybe I should have explained that to you earlier."

Dmitri just flashed her his wicked grin. "Oh, I can read your subtext perfectly well. Now close your pretty mouth for me, hmm?"

"Argh!"

As exclamations went, it wasn't particularly eloquent, but Reggie thought it summed up her frustration nicely. She tried to think up something more descriptive and withering to shout at Dmitri's back when he leaned down to retrieve something else from the duffle bag. After the last incident, she expected an iron maiden, or maybe a cattle prod (so what if they would never have fit! She was having a moment of hysteria, here!). Instead, when Dmitri sat up, he held two richly colored silk scarves in his hands.

"Isn't it a little late for those?" she asked, not caring if enough venom dripped from her tongue to put an asp to shame. "In case you hadn't noticed, I'm already tied up."

"Oh, I noticed." He stood to get a better view and looked down at her with an expression of purely male satisfaction etched on his face. "You are a glorious sight, *nenagyladnaya*, you at whom I could never tire of looking. But you are still not in the right frame of mind for our time together. I believe this will help."

Reggie would have glared up at him, but apparently Dmitri's adjustment to their little scene involved using one of the silk scarves to blindfold her. The dark, paisley printed cloth cut off her vision entirely, though Dmitri carefully examined the position of the layered material along her brow and her cheeks and beside her nose to be sure no gaps or holes allowed light to seep beneath.

"There. How is that, *milka*?"

"Just peachy."

Dmitri chuckled. "Good. Then be a good girl and lie perfectly still for me."

"Well, since I can't reach the phone to dial 9-1-1, I guess I don't have much choice, do I?"

Reggie was all set to work up a bloody scream the instant she felt the touch of the leather flogger against her skin. Instead, what came out of her mouth ranked somewhere between a whimper and a gasp of pure surprise. Rather than the sting of harsh leather, Reggie's skin jumped at the feel of soft, silky feathers caressing her stomach.

You always have a choice, milaya.

The words whispered through her, less a sound than a knowing, and Reggie groaned. *Damn it, he's doing it again.*

The feather tickled her stomach below the hem of the corset, dipped into the crease between hip and thigh and swirled in teasing circles down toward her aching pussy, half an inch at a time. *How can I be doing it again when I have barely started?*

I don't know how you're doing it in the first place!

Her abdominal muscles clenched against the sensations racing though them, and Reggie shook her head to clear it. The idea of being tied down and at the mercy of a strange man freaked her out quite enough. Being tied down and at the mercy of a strange man with supernatural abilities might just be too much for her to handle.

You can handle more than you think, dushka. *And you will.*

The feathery touch withdrew long enough to let her take a breath, but not long enough that she could brace herself before it returned, this time stroking softly against the underside of her breast. It felt different this time, though. Before, the sensation had been like a ghosting on her skin, gone without a trace, so if she had been alone (and not tied up), she would have wondered if she'd imagined it. This time the feathers, though just as soft, seemed to leave an echo of their touch on the skin beneath her left breast even as they moved on to the right.

"What are you doing?" she gasped, her back arching involuntarily to press her skin against the phantom touch.

He didn't answer—at least, not verbally. But the very next thing to pierce her consciousness was the warm, damp glide of his tongue along the skin where the feather had dusted.

"Oh! What—?" She broke off at the feel of the feathers tickling her mouth. When they pulled away, she instinctively licked her lips. She felt the fine grit of dust for a split second before the texture melted against her tongue, leaving her with the warm, sweet taste of honey in her mouth.

It is almost as sweet as your skin, milka. *But I think you taste even better on your own.*

His tongue flicked out in a last, brief caress to the heavy curve of her right breast. All at once, he lowered his head and drew one taut, dusky nipple deep into his mouth.

"Ah," she groaned while the meaning of her life distilled down to that one moment and the sensation of Dmitri sucking at her breast.

His mouth felt like a furnace against her skin, and he drew on her flesh with strong, rhythmic pulls. She tried to reach down to him, to cradle his head in her hands, but she only succeeded in tugging hard at the silken ropes that bound her. Frustrated, she groaned even louder and arched closer to him. His mouth felt wonderful—better than wonderful—but the attention to her breasts only made her cunt throb in time to his sucking.

His teeth closed around her nipple. *Perfectly still, milaya. Be a good girl for me.*

"Misha," she began, her voice faintly pleading. "Please…"

Aren't I pleasing you? Even in her mind she could hear the amused note in his words, and she scowled.

"Tease."

Dmitri chuckled, pulling his mouth from her breast with a hollow pop. He left her only long enough to trace a path across her chest and to her other nipple. He latched on with evident greed, and Reggie moaned, her hands clenching and releasing uselessly above her head.

Am I teasing you, dushka?

One strong, long-fingered hand began to attend to her abandoned nipple, caressing the nubby areole before taking the swollen tip between finger and thumb and pinching a little less than gently.

"Ah! Yes, Misha. Please. O-oh!"

She felt his mouth leave her aching breast, felt the loss of his heat when he drew back from her. Yet his fingers continued to play with her puckered nipple, pinching and rolling the swollen nub.

Even with the blindfold on, she sensed his eyes on her. His gaze itself touched her, caressed her like another hand. She felt it on her face and her breast, and she shivered.

"You like that," he murmured aloud this time, more an observation than a question, but she couldn't muffle her breathless whimper of response.

His fingers tightened further, sending sharp stingers of pleasure-pain along that unique pathway of sensation that ran from her breasts to her pussy.

"Yes!" She gasped it, fighting against her bonds, fighting to feel more of him. "Please, Misha, more."

"So polite," he murmured. "Such a good little girl you sound, *milaya.* Are you really a good little girl?"

Reggie could barely remember her name and he expected her to answer questions?

"Yes...anything. Whatever you want, Misha. Just, please. More."

If anything, his fingers softened around her nipple, making her whimper in frustration. He was doing it again. He had made her so hot, and now he was pulling away!

That thought echoed in her head for about three milliseconds before it—and every other conscious thought she had managed to come by—flew out of her head, pushed aside by the sensation of his long, thick finger parting her soft folds and penetrating her.

It felt so good, so much better than the phantom hands he'd touched her with before. This time the touch felt real and solid and hot against her wet tissues. She couldn't help it. A low keening cry burst from her lips, and her hips jerked sharply upward to envelope his invading digit as deeply as possible. "Misha!"

His hand smacked her sharply on the flank. She heard the cracking sound of it before she felt the impact, but the sting sent her hips pressing back to the mattress.

"Ow!"

"I told you twice not to move, Regina."

His voice sounded firm and forbidding, but somehow Reggie didn't feel frightened. In fact, even with his rough pinch of her nipples and the firm spank he'd just given her, Reggie still wasn't afraid.

Because you trust me, dushka. *As you should*. His words sounded tender and patient, definitely a contrast with his last spoken commands and with his outward manner. Reggie hadn't thought it was trust she felt when he'd pointed that silicone baseball bat of a dildo her way, and it certainly hadn't been what she'd felt when he'd overwhelmed her with that magic hands trick.

A moment of panic, he dismissed. *Natural, really. You were not ready to experience that forbidden fantasy of yours. And the toys were not what you wanted.* He flicked his thumb against her firm little clit to make her gasp, and inserted a second finger into her slick cunt. *This is what you wanted.*

The width of the two digits stretched her, reminding her of how long it had been since she'd had sex. She felt full and somehow more spread and exposed than being tied mostly naked to the bedposts had managed.

"This is what you want, isn't it, *dushka*?"

She couldn't think clearly. She couldn't even tell the difference between his voice in her head and in her ears. It didn't matter anymore. The only thing that mattered was that he keep touching her. That he fuck her.

"Isn't it, Regina?"

He punctuated the repeated question with a twist of his wrist, sending his fingers even deeper inside her, rubbing against her slick, sensitive inner flesh.

"Yes!"

She hoped that was the right answer, because it was probably the most coherent reply she could manage.

"Yes, what, Regina?"

Oh, God, don't make me think! Make me come! Can't think — can't… Ah! Uhn…more…

His fingers pinched her nipple tightly and lifted, tugging hard at the beaded peak. A flash of pain tried to register in her hazed mind, but it blended with the pleasure and became just another level of the sensation that overwhelmed her. She moaned.

"Yes, what, Regina?" His fingers pumped inside her pussy, the way made slick and smooth by her wetness.

Crooking his index finger, he scraped the nail carefully against her inner wall. "Yes, you want this?"

"Yes. This! God, Misha—" Her head flew back against the pillow, her muscles clenched and straining with the pleasure. "Anything. Anything you want, Misha. Please!"

She was too far gone to sense his presence when he leaned close to her, but she felt his breath whisper against her ear.

"And if I want you to beg, *dushka*?"

His purring rumble shot through her, combining with the erotic imagery of his words to make her jerk and tremble beneath him.

"Yes, please," she whispered, her voice becoming as husky and intense as his. "I'll beg. I'll do anything, Misha. Anything you want. But please, please fuck me."

She arched her back, pressing her nipple into his palm and her hips into his hand, pushing her cunt against his fingers. Her muscles clenched, squeezing as if it were his cock filling her.

"Misha, please fuck me."

All at once, she felt his weight lever away from her, and she couldn't suppress a distressed whimper.

Hush.

Before she worked up a full-fledged protest, she felt his hands on the silk that covered her eyes. The scarf loosened and fell away, and Reggie blinked against the soft light of her bedside lamp. Her vision focused enough to make out Dmitri's hard, muscular chest, and her eyes were closing again when he lowered his mouth to hers.

It was the first time he had kissed her, and Reggie knew the moment would be frozen in her mind for a very long time. He wasted no time courting her mouth, offered no deference to the newness of the experience. He devoured her, his lips covering hers, teeth nipping, tongue invading. He kissed as if he would swallow her, take her inside himself, as she prepared to take him inside of her.

The kiss made her resent her bonds. She wished fervently her arms were free to wrap around his broad shoulders, that she could run her fingers though his soft, dark hair. She wished her legs were free to wrap around his waist and urge him inside her.

Please, Dmitri. I can't wait anymore. Please fuck me now.

He responded before she finished the thought. She felt the blunt, round head of his cock press through her slit and lodge against the entrance to her aching cunt.

She heard his voice in her mind. *Open for me*, milka. *Open wide for me in welcome.*

And then she heard nothing.

In that moment, her cunt became her entire existence. Her world centered on the soft, wet channel between her legs and the thick, hard cock that demanded entrance.

She felt that first time hesitation, the heightened tension and the sense of wonder at the ability of her body to stretch apart for a man, to take him inside of her and give him pleasure. She felt the sensation of stretching and the brief doubt about whether or not her body would accommodate his. With Dmitri, she felt right to wonder.

His cock pressed hard against her opening and Reggie froze, waiting for the burning sensation to ease. She felt an internal pop when the head breached her entrance and expected the dulling of sensation that usually followed. Instead, her body stretched further when Dmitri began to force his length even deeper.

The shaft of his cock felt hot and smooth and thick as it tunneled inside her, at least as thick as the head. Instead of the stretching sensation easing, it grew even more intense with every inch he pressed inside her.

Reggie whimpered and shifted her hips, looking for a break from the intensity of the sensation, but Dmitri grew ruthless. His hands reached down to grasp her hips, forcing her high and hard against him. He held her so tightly she knew his fingertips would leave bruises where they dug into her flesh.

"Uhn! I can't...I— Ah! Dmitri, please. No more!" Her head tossed wildly against the pillow, her eyes clenched shut, her brow furrowed in distress. She tugged against the cords around her wrist as if she could climb up and away from him. She would die if he stopped, but she didn't know if she could bear for him to continue.

"Yes. More. Look at me." He rasped the words through gritted teeth.

Reggie struggled to obey. She pulled harder at the silk cords to distract herself while she tried to force her eyelids to lift. When she had managed slits, she caught sight of Dmitri above her and almost snapped them closed again. His eyes burned with heat and lust, and his normally harsh features might have been carved from dark granite.

"Take me," he growled, shoving another inch into her distressed cunt. "Take all of me."

Reggie gasped, squirming beneath him, using her grip on the cords to try to pull herself away from him. "I can't! Misha, please."

He only gripped her hips tighter and thrust deeper. "All of me."

And with one mighty lunge, he buried his entire length in her grasping pussy.

She screamed.

She felt as if he had split her in two. He felt so huge, so much bigger than anything she'd ever experienced, and so much harder. His cock stretched her until she thought she couldn't stand it, and his hard hips pressed into hers and forced her pelvis flat against the mattress. When he started thrusting, he would kill her.

He started thrusting.

Instead of ripping her apart like she'd feared, the intense pleasure-pain of the friction set off a chain reaction inside her. Her cunt clenched around his cock, her muscles clenched against the cords, and her nipples clenched into painfully tight buds where they rubbed against his broad chest.

Instead of trying to draw away, she threw herself at him, flinging her hips up to meet his thrusts, bucking wildly beneath him, while sounds she'd never heard before escaped her lips. She moaned, she panted, she squealed and through it all, she begged him to fuck her harder.

"More! Misha, please. Harder!"

He grunted and fucked her harder. His weight lowered onto her, pinning her to the mattress and holding her in place for his thrusts. His arms slipped beneath hers and clamped onto her shoulders, pressing her body hard into his pounding thrusts.

Her entire body clenched. Her neck bowed, shoving her head back into her pillow. Her body arched beneath him, trying to fuse them together so she would never be empty again.

He moved in a blur of motion, racing with her toward orgasm. Her pussy fluttered around him, and he groaned. He lowered his head, and she felt his forehead press against her chest. A thin sheen of moisture slicked both their skins, and they rubbed together so hotly she knew they would spark at any moment.

Harder and harder he thrust, faster and faster until she couldn't hope to keep pace. She stopped moving and instead, braced her feet against the mattress and held her hips high and hard against his. His thrusts became shorter and faster, and he rubbed hard against her clit with every motion. The tension coiled inside her, and she choked on her own breath.

Her pussy clamped down hard until he had to force his cock free of her grasping muscles.

"Come for me," he grunted. "Now."

With a shriek, she obeyed. Her mind went blank, and she swore her heart stopped. Her cunt spasmed hard around his cock. The pleasure ripped through her, as brutal as their mating itself, wringing her of all feeling until she collapsed limp beneath him.

Three short, hard thrusts later he followed, shouting his pleasure to the ceiling while he pumped her full of his semen.

Reggie lay motionless, waiting for awareness and sensation to return to her well-used body.

My God. I think I'm dead, she mused, too tired to get worked up about it. *He fucked me to death.*

Not yet, milaya, he chuckled. *But there's always next time.*

Chapter Six

Dmitri lay on his side, watching Regina sleep. After their first intense mating, he had quickly untied her bonds and removed her confining corset. Nude and exhausted, she had settled close, curling her soft, warm frame against his side and slipping into sleep as easily as a toddler.

That had been hours ago, and ignoring his renewed hunger for her had become almost impossible.

He brushed a silky tendril of hair off of her cheek, rubbing his knuckles against the velvet-smooth surface of her skin. He'd never seen anything so beautiful as his Regina, naked and bound, or naked and orgasmic, or naked and asleep, with her knees curled up toward her chest and her hands pillowed beneath her cheek.

He felt an intense sense of satisfaction at having made her his. While the hunt had been brief, he felt none of the boredom that usually followed close on the heels of a conquest. Instead of feeling sated with her, he'd found possessing her only whetted his appetite. Hence, the enormous erection he sported at that very moment.

Shifting closer to her, Dmitri curled around Regina's body and wrapped his arm about her, resting his palm flat against her pelvis. He pressed her back against his hips until his cock nestled between her ass cheeks.

She murmured something unintelligible and shifted against him. Finding a comfortable spot, she drifted back to sleep.

Dmitri savored the feel of her body in his arms. He nuzzled his face against her neck, breathing deeply of her scent. She smelled of honey and musk and desire, the warmth of her skin carrying the scent to his appreciative nose. Good enough to eat, and Dmitri suddenly felt very hungry.

His tongue traced the shell of her ear, teased the small hollow below, and she rewarded him with a sleepy murmur of pleasure. His arms wrapped more tightly around her, the hand on her stomach tilting her pelvis back against him while he lifted her leg in his other hand and draped her thigh on top of his. She sighed and tilted her head slightly to give him better access while he nibbled his way down her throat to the warm, scented curve where her neck met her shoulder.

"Misha."

She whispered his name in her sleep, and he growled, a low, possessive rumble of triumph and lust. He had to have her again.

His hand slid from her thigh up to cup around her breast. He squeezed the soft weight, pinching his fingers around the nipple and causing it to harden into a rosy nub. She murmured and pressed back against him.

He arched her hips further, canting them up until he could nudge his cock against her entrance. His hand slid down, combing through her neatly trimmed bush to delve into her slit. Her pussy lips parted softly for him, and he tested her readiness with the tips of his first two fingers. She dripped with arousal, more than ready for his possession. He shifted his hand up until it cupped over her lower stomach, only the tip of the middle finger still parting her and pressing against her clit.

He pinched her nipple hard between thumb and finger, simultaneously pressing down on her clit and breaching her tender pussy with his cock.

He knew the instant when she woke, felt her tense around him and whimper, her cunt clenching while its abraded walls tried to relax enough to admit his cock. He watched her face carefully, searching for signs of real distress. Her brow furrowed, though her eyes never opened, and she bit her lower lip, her skin flushing delicately. She made no move to stop him, so he continued, patiently but inexorably forcing his cock in her to the hilt. She moaned.

"Easy, *dushka*," he whispered, kissing the side of her neck and rubbing small circles around her clit. "You can take me. Slowly, slowly. That's my girl."

When he slowed to a stop, her cunt rippled around him and eased, hugging his cock in a silky, wet embrace.

"Misha."

He kissed her temple and touched his tongue to the dark curve of her lashes resting against her cheek. He cupped her breast and her cunt closer against him and began to move.

He eased his cock in and out of her with long, smooth strokes, loving the way she clasped about him, the tightness of her pussy like a virgin's surrounding him. He knew it had been several months since she'd broken up with some little insect of a man who polluted her mind like an oil spill, and from reading her thoughts, he knew they had ceased to be intimate long before the relationship ended. Judging by the way she closed so tightly around him, he guessed she had taken no other man to her bed since.

The thought gave him a savage sense of satisfaction. He hated that Regina had ever taken another man into her body, but now he would make sure he was the last who would ever feel her warm, welcoming pussy.

Concentrating on the pleasure she gave him, Dmitri quickened his thrusts, urging his cock more forcefully into her. She whimpered, reaching one arm back to curl around his neck, holding him close to her. She turned her head and parted her lips, rooting blindly for his kiss.

He took her mouth as he took her body, with gentle force, ruthless control and an overwhelming sense of inevitability. He adored the taste of her, sweet and warm and spicy, like honey and cinnamon and the unique flavor that was Regina. He teased her tongue and tickled the roof of her mouth, urging her to play with him. She responded eagerly, sucking at his tongue, drawing him deeply within her, just as she drew his cock into her tight heat. Dmitri groaned low in his throat, the sound like a growl, and thrust his hips harder against her.

Reggie tore her mouth away from his and turned her face to muffle her moans of pleasure in her pillow. Dmitri pulled it out from under her and scowled.

"No," he rumbled, sliding his hands to her hips and rolling her onto her belly. "You will not hide the sounds of your pleasure from me. I will hear every breath and every moan I wring from you. Do you understand?"

Reggie braced her hands against the mattress and moaned, tilting her hips to try and take more of him. "Yes, Misha," she whimpered. "I understand."

He grunted a response, grabbed her pillow and his and lifted her hips to slide the support beneath her. The pillows tilted her hips up toward him, and Dmitri's eyes narrowed in satisfaction at the sight of her bottom elevated for his possession.

He thrust faster into her, draping his weight along her back to pin her to the mattress. His next deep thrust bumped hard against her cervix, and Reggie's control snapped. She came, moaning and bucking beneath him.

Dmitri grabbed hard onto her hips and rode out her pleasure, his face buried in the curve of her shoulder. He could hear her pulse beating frantically just beneath her skin, could smell her excitement and her pleasure and the rich scent of her life, warm and vital.

Hunger stirred in him, and he groaned. He had struggled with his desire to taste her during their first, furious mating, but now it surged to life with twice the insistence. He needed to mark her, to take her life force inside of him until she could never part from him again.

Resolute, he slowed his movements inside her just enough to allow him to focus his thoughts on hers. He entered her mind much more gently than he entered her body, less sure of his welcome. She didn't seem to notice, too wrapped up in her physical senses to attend to her others. It made things much easier for him while he drew a gentle veil over her consciousness. He wanted her to remain tangled in the moment, but not to remember what he was about to do.

When he felt sure she knew nothing else but the feel of his body inside hers, he draped his hard frame over her back and quickened his rhythm, pressing his hips harder against her.

Her spasming cunt drove him wild, and he gave in to his need. With his hips hammering into her with animal savagery, he opened his lips against the tender skin at the seam of her shoulder and sank his fangs into her sweet, pale flesh. He fed, oblivious to all but the taste of her blood in his mouth, the feel of her skin and her flesh and her hot, tight cunt.

He drew from her like a starving man. The taste of her filled him, overwhelmed him. Sweeter than the honey, hotter than her passion, her blood nourished him like nothing ever had. He felt drunk on her essence, the life of her intoxicating him like vodka, but sweeter, clearer, more pure. He feared he would never have enough of her, and the thought pierced the fog of his lust. He drew back, his body clenching above hers while her taste overwhelmed him.

He came on a roar, the cry filling the room and echoing off the walls. He pumped his semen into her until he emptied himself and collapsed on top of her, struggling to catch his breath.

She was glorious.

When he regained control of his muscles, Dmitri brushed her hair away from the damp skin of her neck and kissed the spot he'd bitten with reverent tenderness. She remained motionless, and he knew the veil over his actions had held. He murmured her name.

"Regina."

She sighed and shifted, but made no response. She'd fallen back to sleep.

Dmitri chuckled, unsure if he should be flattered or insulted. Gently disengaging their bodies, he scowled at the loss of her wet heat surrounding him. If he could simply stay inside her for the rest of eternity, Dmitri figured he would live a very happy life.

A glance at the clock told him dawn would come soon, and he sighed. He knew he would have to leave her. He could think of nothing more appealing than remaining in her bed and holding her for the rest of the night and all of the next day, but she would not find it easy to adjust to his lifestyle, and he knew crowding her too quickly would likely send her running from him. He would never allow that to happen.

He sat up in her bed and stretched muscles that ached pleasantly from his exertion. He should leave her before the sight of her tempted him to further exercise.

He kissed her tenderly on the cheek, grinning when she grumbled in her sleep and curled away from him. He had worn her out, and she obviously refused to let him interrupt her sleep for sex yet again.

He had no plans to wake her, no matter how his libido urged him to do so. He would let her sleep for now. He could afford such generosity, because he knew it would not be long before he saw her again.

Brushing her tangled hair off her cheek, he let his hand cup the side of her face while he gazed down at her and slipped his mind into hers. He double checked his veil and found no trace of memory lingering to tell her what he was or that he had fed from her while they made love. All she could remember would be passion and pleasure.

He had to resist the urge to give the pleasure memories an extra boost, just to be safe. Instead, he gave her the thought that he desired her as much as she desired him, that he could not wait to see her again. He molded the thought until it took the proportion of memory, and he could be certain she would heed it. He kissed her once more and stood.

He took a few moments to straighten up, pulling the disarranged sheets back onto the mattress and smoothing them down, tucking Regina inside. He wound up the cords and the blindfold he'd used on her and put away all the other accoutrements of their encounter. If he hadn't known Reggie's friends had provided her with these things, he'd have gotten a very different impression of her, he thought, grinning. Reading her mind definitely made things easier.

When the room looked tidy, he pulled on his jeans, draped his shirt over his shoulder and carried his boots into her living room. He snooped just enough to find one of her business cards, which he pocketed before he finished dressing and let himself quietly out of her apartment. Now that he knew where she worked, he would be able to keep tabs on her during the week while he dedicated his attention to clearing a path for their relationship.

It grated at him, the thought of the small steps he would have to endure while he worked to overcome her natural suspicions of him. He hated the time it would take, wanted to make her officially his, but he would have things settled so no one could doubt Regina belonged to him — not even Regina.

Chapter Seven

Reggie woke Saturday morning with a song in her heart and an ache between her thighs.

Eyes snapping open, she flew into a sitting position in the middle of her big bed and surveyed the room around her. It looked like he'd never been there.

She blinked, but everything appeared perfectly normal. The room was neat and bright in the light flooding through the two casement windows. She didn't know what she'd been expecting to see, given they'd confined their activities to the bed the entire time, but there should have been *something*. Surely the most amazing night of her life would leave her with some kind of reminder?

Then she stretched, and she discovered exactly where the reminder came from; it lurked in her muscles — every single one of them. She ached from her neck down, remnants of the bondage as much as the enthusiastic sex. Bringing her arms back to her sides, she rolled her shoulders to loosen the tight muscles and absently rubbed her wrists. They bore no marks, no sign of the ropes that had held her still and spread for Dmitri, but she could still feel them against her skin. She did find marks on her hips, though, dusky impressions that showed where his fingers had bitten into her flesh while he held her still and fucked her.

God! What a night!

With a heartfelt sigh, Reggie swung her legs over the side of the bed, stood and failed to suppress a wince. She hobbled, as bowlegged as a drunken cowboy, into the adjoining bathroom and turned the shower on to hot.

Once the pelting water had loosened the worst of her knotted muscles, she shampooed her hair and lathered a loofah with her favorite honeysuckle-scented soap. The familiar fragrance brought memory flooding back.

I love your scent, milaya. *Like honey and musk and warm, wet woman.*

Even in the heat of the shower, the memory made her shiver. She wondered what would happen when she actually saw him again. The man would be lucky if she didn't trip him and beat him to the floor…

She froze. It seemed weird, but she knew she would indeed see him again. Despite the fact that she'd woken up alone in her bed with not a hair out of place and not a scrap of evidence to prove Dmitri Vidâme even existed, she never doubted he would come back to her. Her mind tried to logic it out, saying she didn't know where he lived, what he did, or even if that was his real name, but she didn't care. She knew with an unshakeable faith her time with Dmitri had been more than a one-night stand.

Operating on autopilot, her mind otherwise occupied, she finished up her shower, wrapped herself in a bath sheet and headed into the kitchen. She was starving. Apparently, being fucked within an inch of her life by a mysterious man with psychic powers could really work up an appetite.

She rummaged around for some food while the coffee brewed. Cereal wouldn't cut it this morning. She held two eggs and a carton of milk when the phone rang, and of course, by the time she managed to set them down without cracking the eggs, her machine had picked up.

Reggie reached for the receiver, but yanked her hand back when she heard the voice on the answering machine's speaker.

"Reggie, it's Ava. If you're there, pick up." Pause. "I'm going to assume that you're exhausted and still asleep, but if I don't hear from you by this afternoon, I'm going to call the police. Call me."

The machine clicked and beeped when the call ended, and the recording stopped. Reggie groaned and groaned again when she saw the rapidly blinking light indicating she had more messages waiting. Bracing herself, she pushed play. All of the messages were from Ava.

Beep. "You better have a damn good reason for sneaking out of the club, Regina Elaina McNeill!" Ava must have called on her cell last night, because Reggie could hear the noise of the club in the background. "Just wait until I get my hands on you!"

Beep. "All right, you get slightly less painful revenge. Missy just said she saw you leave with someone gorgeous. Of course, we have no way of knowing he's not a serial killer until you *call and let us know you're okay!*"

Beep. "The club's closing in a few and no call. Where are you? You'd better be okay, or I'll kill you myself."

Beep. "We checked with the bartender, since no one has heard from you, and he said you left with a man named Dmitri, who he guaranteed was not a psycho ax maniac. He'd better be right, and you'd better call as soon as you wake up. Good-night."

Reggie rolled her eyes at the machine and hit the delete button. She knew her friends only wanted to make sure she was okay, but their attitude rankled, especially after they had gotten her into the situation to begin with. If not for their Fix, Reggie would never have gone to that club, let alone have left with a total stranger, god-like sex appeal or no.

She glanced over at the clock and did some quick calculations. Saturday at eleven meant Missy would be at the park with her niece and nephew and would check her cell for messages in precisely half an hour, just before she took the kids out for lunch. Telling herself "prudent" sounded better than "cowardly," Reggie dismissed the idea of calling Ava and dialed Missy's cell. When the message ended and the voice mail program beeped at her, Reggie spoke.

"Hi, it's me. I got a bunch of messages from Ava on my machine. I just wanted to let everyone know I'm fine. I had a great time last night, but I've got a ton of chores to catch up on today, so I might not talk to ya'll until Monday. Give Nicky and Beth hugs for me. Bye."

After she hung up the phone, she pushed Ava from her mind and focused on the really important things. Like food.

An hour later, fortified with an omelet and coffee and decently dressed in a pair of faded jeans and a knit top, Reggie made good on her lie and got down to cleaning her apartment. Not being a total slob or an unmarried man, it went quickly.

When the phone rang an hour later, she almost missed it over the dull roar of the vacuum cleaner. As it was, she barely got to the receiver before the machine picked up.

"Hello?" She knew she sounded breathless, but that's what happened when someone called on cleaning day. They'd have to deal.

"Reggie?"

Okay, what higher power have I pissed off this week? Reggie wondered while she sank to the arm of the chair beside her and took a deep breath. "Hello, Greg."

"I was hoping I'd catch you at home. How've you been?"

You mean, since I caught you debriefing your administrative assistant on your lunch hour? Or can you not debrief someone who's wearing a thong? "Just fine, thanks."

"Good, good." He sounded just a little nervous, which made Reggie's day just a little brighter. "Listen, I know you probably aren't all that thrilled with me these days—"

Gee, do you think, Einstein? "Don't be silly."

"But I'd really like to see you. Do you think there's any chance you might consider meeting me for a drink somewhere?"

Whoa. That brought her up short. Gutless Greg the Wunderjerk wanted to see her again? For what? Did he really think she wanted to hear his lame explanations all over again? Did he think it would make the slightest bit of difference if he finally apologized? If he begged for forgiveness? If he got down on his hands and knees and groveled before her feet like the immoral dog he was? Okay, so maybe that last bit would help. She sure enjoyed the imagery. "When did you have in mind?"

"Tonight?"

What? Did he not think she might possibly have other plans on a Saturday night? Just because she didn't was no reason to assume anything.

"Unless you already have plans."

"Well, I do have something planned," she lied, her tone purposefully cool and bored, "but I might be able to spare you twenty minutes or so if you could make it early enough. Say, six-thirty? Let me check my calendar."

She made a big production of flipping through the calendar she kept beside the phone, hoping the sound of the pages turning would carry over the phone lines. She scrolled her finger down the list of errands she'd recorded there and tried to sound breezy.

"Yes, I think I could squeeze you in around six-thirty, but I have to —"

The words caught in her throat when her finger reached the bottom of the page and slid across the unfamiliar handwriting. Written in bold strokes across the white, lined page, she read, "Captain Jack's, 8 pm. Wear the red."

Dmitri. She didn't need to recognize his handwriting to know who had written himself so matter-of-factly into her schedule. Into her life.

"Six-thirty is perfect," Greg said, shaking her out of her stupor. His voice actually sounded almost relieved and excited at the same time. "I could meet you at that place right down the street from you. Captain Morgan's?"

"Captain Jack's," she corrected, dazed.

"Right, that one. I'll see you there at six-thirty." He paused. "Thanks for agreeing to this, Reg. I appreciate you making the time to talk to me after what happened."

Reggie muttered something even she didn't understand and hung up the phone with numb fingers. Her mind had already evicted Gregory and busied itself with unpacking Dmitri's suitcases and tucking his slippers under her bed. Apparently her gut feeling in the shower had been right. She would be seeing Dmitri again, and sooner than she'd thought. Like tonight.

Wear the red.

Feeling uneasy, as if someone watched her from the corner, Reggie dropped the vacuum and headed for her closet. Reaching inside, she rummaged into the very back and pulled out a sealed garment bag. Her hands ripped open the dark plastic covering and smoothed over the velvet material of the dress it concealed.

Short, tight and unrepentantly crimson, she hadn't ever actually worn the dress. She'd bought it for the holidays last year, planned to wear it to spice things up with Greg, but that was B.L. — before Lisette. Instead, she'd had it cleaned unnecessarily and sealed it away in the back of her closet like another bad memory. She'd forgotten she owned it, until Dmitri reminded her.

Wear the red.

He meant this dress; she didn't own any others in red. With her auburn hair, she tended to think the color clashed, so she avoided it as a general rule. The contents of this garment bag were the exception. But how had he known about it? The bag had been sealed and still hidden where she'd last put it.

The man reads your mind, and you wonder how he knew you owned a red dress? she asked herself, then answered with a frustrated, *I was trying not to think about the mind reading thing.*

Collapsing onto the bed beside the red dress, Reggie groaned. She used to live a nice, ordinary life. Honest. She worked at an ad firm, she hung out with her friends, she dated a financial analyst and she had never let anyone tie her up. But then her boyfriend turned out to be a cheating scum sucker, her friends lost their minds and turned into sex-yentas from hell, and she hooked up with a man who read her mind and persuaded her to reenact the Pornographic Perils of Pauline.

At least the job's still normal.

"Yeah, I'm the one who's losing it," she sighed, finally admitting it out loud. She should probably resign herself to life in a padded cell.

Nothing so drastic. Perhaps merely velvet-lined handcuffs.

The purring voice inside her head sounded so familiar and so impossible Reggie offered the only logical response. She screamed.

Hush, milaya, *or someone will think you are being murdered.* His voice, impossible as it sounded, laughed at her from inside her mind, and Reggie wondered how this was meant to convince her of her sanity?

Though perhaps they will just think your companion from last night is visiting you again.

"Very funny," Reggie snapped, glaring into the thin air that Dmitri did *not* occupy. "Where are you, and why are you trying to turn my life into an episode of the *Twilight Zone*?"

He chuckled. It felt like her brain vibrated.

I am at home, milaya. *And I am here with you. Have you missed me?*

"Not as much as my sanity."

You are not crazy, Regina, just a bit too focused on what you believe to be real and imaginary. I will enjoy opening your eyes to new...possibilities.

"Will you stop that? Enough with the double entendre. Or was that a triple entendre?"

It was a promise.

Reggie rolled her eyes, jumped up off the bed, faced thin air, since Misha was still *not* there, and growled, "That's it, buddy. Get out of my head and stay out! We are going to lay this down in person, using noises and vocal chords and all sorts of wacky social conventions. Whatever you had planned for tonight can wait until you give me some answers. Now, go *away*!"

He left with a chuckle, but leave he did. Reggie experienced the removal of his presence from her mind like a physical withdrawal and fought not to clench her thighs together.

"Jerk." She snarled the insult and, lacking a certain arrogant Russian to clobber, slammed her closet door shut. "That tears it. Men are just pigs. All men. Every single sleazy, sex-obsessed, lesbian-fantasy-perpetuating, sports-show-watching, big-breast-ogling, secretary-screwing one of them!"

Furious, she came an inch away from consigning Dmitri to the same fiery pit of abhorrence Greg had fallen into, but she couldn't make herself do it. Not yet anyway. She felt obligated to give the man a few more than eighteen hours to prove himself. Greg wore the label "lost cause" stamped on his forehead, but she might be able to salvage Dmitri.

With that thought in mind, a slow, wicked smile spread across Reggie's face and a plan bloomed in her consciousness. Maybe this evening she could finally make Greg pay; and if Dmitri squirmed…well, that would just be icing.

She took another look at the velvet dress and an idea filled her mind. A very wicked, very naughty, very dangerous idea.

Carefully, she hung the dress back in the closet, and propped the door open wide to reveal the full length mirror that hung on the inside panel. She stepped backward to the bed, making sure she stayed in sight of her reflected image.

If Dmitri was so determined to poke around in her mind, she might as well make sure he found something worth his while.

When the back of her knees bumped against her mattress, she closed her eyes and concentrated.

At first, she didn't even know what she was doing. She just kept her eyes closed and her mind blank and concentrated on the rhythmic pulse of her breath, in and out. When the last idle thought left her mind, she cast a mental look around to see what she might find.

She found traces of Dmitri everywhere, the echoing memory of her time with him. She examined those memories, but found them disconnected and unhelpful. She hesitated a moment, unsure of what she looked for, until she found it.

At the edge of her mind, she found a piece of him waiting, a fresh piece where he'd touched her mind a few minutes ago before she had ordered him to go away. She touched that piece and found it had the feel of his skin, hot and smooth and tingling with energy.

With a silent thanks to her years of meditation and yoga classes, Reggie grasped that piece in her mind's hands and shifted it between them until she found the cord that bound it to its source.

A cord led her down an unfamiliar path, one she'd never seen before, and when her feet stepped along the mental corridor she knew Dmitri had recently laid it by linking his mind to hers. She knew he wouldn't have been careless enough to leave it unless he wanted her to follow it. She couldn't have found him on her own, not being Mr. Psychic Phenomenon like some people, but with the trail to follow she hesitantly made her way down the path that linked her mind to his.

She had some really great, subtle plans laid for sneaking up on him and staging a mental ambush, but the instant her mind slipped into his, she heard him chuckle.

What's so funny? she scowled.

You are, milka. *You could not sneak up on a herd of deaf elephants, let alone on me. You don't have my powers, and you cannot hope to use them against me.*

She heard his voice in her mind, rumbling and amused, and she decided to unveil her secret weapon.

I don't need to sneak up on you, she thought. *I have other things I can use against you much more effectively.*

And with that, she opened her eyes, stared into her mirror and stripped off her jeans.

She felt his indrawn breath, felt the sudden stillness of his mental presence. She knew what she saw filled her mind and therefore filled his as well.

Because he'd ordered it last night, she wore no panties beneath her jeans. When she pushed them off her hips and let them fall to the floor, she bared herself to their shared sight. She felt him tense, and even though she couldn't see where he was, couldn't sense his body as she knew he could hers, she knew she had his undivided attention.

Smiling in wicked satisfaction, she ran her palms up the length of her smooth thighs, pressing the backs of her hands together and slipping them between her legs. Her forefingers tickled her tender pussy lips, and she spread her legs further while she stroked the tender surface of her inner thighs.

She dwelled on every sensation, just to torture him. Since he wasn't there in person, he couldn't interfere, couldn't stop her from doing exactly as she pleased, and she relished the control.

Pulling her hands from between her legs, she let them glide over the soft curve of her stomach and up beneath her short, knit top. Grasping the hem in her hands, she tugged the shirt off and threw it onto the floor beside her discarded jeans. Standing in front of her mirror in nothing but a sheer, peach bra and a wide, wicked smile, Reggie let her lover look his fill.

Never before had she stood naked in front of a mirror and felt so sexy. Usually she was too busy cataloging her shortcomings and couldn't see the overall picture. This time she had Dmitri's thoughts tangled up with hers, and she could see herself the way he did. She saw the figure she thought of as twenty pounds too heavy had the ripe, lush curves of a pre-Raphaelite goddess. Her hips begged to receive a man's weight, her thighs to clamp tight around him. Her waist looked tiny in contrast to her full hips and breasts that jutted heavy and proud from her chest. Dmitri loved the sight of her, and that made her beautiful in her own eyes.

Before he could take over completely, Reggie drew her gaze from her breasts and rested it on her hands while they unfastened the front clasp of her bra and let the filmy material fall away. With her mind full of Misha, she slid her hands up her torso and cupped her breasts in her palms.

She overflowed her own small hands, but she remembered the feel of Dmitri's upon her, and she sighed.

Her fingers rubbed over her erect nipples, making the flesh bead more tightly. The peaks stabbed into her palms, and she shifted to grip each nipple between her thumbs and forefingers. She squeezed with gradually increasing pressure until the squeeze became a pinch and the pinch made her moan. Her eyelids drifted down, but she kept them open, not wanting Misha to lose a moment of her sight.

Imagine if you were here with me, she thought, weighing her breasts in her hands and meeting her own gaze in the mirror. She could almost see the faint black shadow of his eyes behind her own. *Imagine if you touched me again, how good it would feel.*

She heard his growl and smiled.

Her fingers closed hard around her nipples, and she shuddered. She left one hand clamped around an aroused nipple, but slid the other down the center of her chest to her pussy. The damp flesh spread open in welcome, and she slid her fingers deep between her legs, brushing over her clit and burrowing between her puffy lips.

Do you remember how I felt, Misha? Was I this wet when you touched me? Because it feels like a river in here.

Her fingers shifted, pressed deeper, found her opening. She circled the tender flesh with the tip of one fingernail and made herself quiver.

That must have been why I was able to take you. You were so big, I thought for a minute that you wouldn't fit, but I wanted you so much. I needed to feel you inside me. Like this.

She pressed two fingers together, fit them to her entrance and drove them deep into her pussy.

She heard him groan.

God! That feels so good, but not as good as your cock. Her eyes were fixed on her image in the mirror, unable to look away from the sight of her hand buried deep between her pale legs. She couldn't see well enough, though, so she withdrew her fingers briefly and pushed herself up onto the edge of her bed, spreading her knees wide and exposing her dripping cunt to the mirror.

Krasavitsa, he groaned. *Beautiful woman.*

Her hand returned to her pussy, parting the drenched folds to reveal her inner secrets to the mirror and to his appreciative eyes. She found the sight fascinated her. She had never examined herself like this, never spread herself open in front of her own eyes and seen what she looked like to a lover.

Her pussy, dark red and plump with swelling, shone with her juices. It stood out in erotic contrast against her pale, slender fingers when she ran them lightly over her damp flesh, feeling the smooth, slick texture.

Do you think I'm beautiful? Her fingers parted into a vee and slid between her labia, scissoring around her firm, little clit and tugging it gently. The rush of sensation made her eyes close for a second, but a growl from Misha sent them opening again.

You are gorgeous, milka, *as you know. But I have warned you about teasing me.*

She smiled and tickled her fingertips against her entrance, scooping up her flowing juices and using them to increase the lubrication. *And what will you do to me, Dmitri? Think me into submission?* Her two fingers slid inside easily, and she tightened her pussy around them, feeling her own internal contractions.

Is this what it feels like when I squeeze your cock, Misha? All soft and tight and slick? She pumped her fingers in and out a few times and moaned, watching the movement in the mirror. Her hand grew slick and shiny from her cunt juice. *Mm, no wonder you like to fuck me. This feels so good.*

The heel of her hand rubbed hard against her clit with every thrust of her fingers, until her hips rocked forward on every stroke. Her other hand lifted to massage her aching breasts, and her eyes closed. She didn't need the mirror when the image of her own hand stroking her quivering pussy had etched itself into her mind.

She fell back against the bed and planted her feet on the edge of the mattress, using the leverage to thrust harder against her penetrating fingers.

She slipped a third digit inside herself and gasped, scraping her fingernails over her puckered nipple while she pleasured herself.

God, Misha, I want you here with me! I need you. I need you inside me.

Her head fell backward, snapping against her shoulders while her entire body arched up from the mattress like a drawn bow. Her fingers thrust hard and carelessly into her cunt, her nails scraping her tender inner tissues, while her thumb pressed hard, rapid circles against her clit.

Her breath stopped and her muscles tensed and her mind reached out to him and her orgasm burst. She came screaming his name, with her eyes squeezed shut and her fingers buried deep in her clenching pussy.

"Misha!"

The spasms shook her for long moments until she collapsed, aching and panting onto her bed. She lay there for several minutes, gasping while her lungs struggled to remember their job. She curled up on her side with her fingers still between her legs, cupped protectively over her sensitive flesh.

So there, she thought sleepily, a smile curving her lips. She felt his continued tension and knew her display had aroused him furiously. *Now you know you're not the only one who can play those little mental games. Maybe you'll be more careful who you eavesdrop on next time.*

The only thing I will be careful of, Regina, he growled at her, enunciating each word clearly as if he spoke through gritted teeth, *is to make sure you get exactly what you deserve. If you tease me like that, you must be prepared to face the consequences.*

Reggie snuggled her cheek into her pillow and yawned delicately. *Consequences, schmonsequences,* she thought. *You couldn't hurt me if you wanted to, you big softy. You're too careful for that.*

I didn't say the consequences would be painful, milaya. *Only that they would be certain. Dream of that.*

And she did. Oh, boy, did she ever.

Chapter Eight

Staring at the contents of her closet, clad only in a towel and her ratty bathrobe, with a glass of wine in her hand, Reggie planned her attack. The crucial first stage involved walking into the bar tonight and making Greg swallow his tongue. Then—maybe—she would think about asking someone to perform the Heimlich, but only if she was feeling generous. And only if it didn't conflict with whatever plans Dmitri had made for them.

She surveyed her arsenal with a critical eye. Part of her wanted to ignore the red dress just because Dmitri had ordered her to wear it, but when she flipped through her wardrobe, she thought it might be her only viable alternative. Plus, she figured after the little performance she'd put on in her mirror, buttering up the man who wanted to make her pay might not be a bad idea.

Still, her contrary nature sent her searching through her closet one last time. Her usual collection of man-magnet dresses didn't pack enough punch, not to mention Greg had seen almost everything she owned. If only she'd reacted to the breakup by shopping, she'd be set, but instead, she'd holed up in her apartment like a hermit. Now, she was paying the price.

Her right hand reached in to flip through hangers, discarding potential outfits, while her left hand brought the glass to her lips for a healthy swallow of wine. Normally, Reggie didn't consider herself a big drinker. Girls' nights were the exception to her behavior rather than the rule, but tonight she'd felt the need for a little liquid courage before braving the upcoming confrontation.

"Boring. Boring. Seen it. Ugh." Mumbling a running commentary on her rejections, Reggie finally reached the end of the closet. She'd left herself with only one choice.

"Damn it." Frowning, she perched on the end of the bed and glowered at the open closet door, as if she could intimidate it into creating new and exciting outfits for her to wear. It didn't happen. She ran her gaze down the entire closet rod one more time, trying to see if she'd missed anything, or if any ideas popped into her head for new ways to combine garments into breathtakingly sexy outfits. No luck. The only things she saw were her own boring old clothes and the red velvet dress that could make a porn star proud. Her salvation had yet to appear.

Reggie drained her glass of wine in disgust and set it aside. Fate decreed she should wear the red dress, and she knew how to give in gracefully. Sort of.

She pulled the dress out of the closet and hooked its hanger over the back of the door. When she stripped away the plastic, the rich sheen of silk velvet caught the light and seemed to breathe. Her hand went out to touch it, drawn by the luxurious promise of the fabric. She'd paid a fortune for the thing, more than she wanted to remember, but in that moment, she decided it had been worth every penny.

Her skin looked pearly-pale where it touched the material, set off against the backdrop of crimson velvet. Instead of washing her out, the color refined her skin to a shade of rich, warm cream that looked smooth enough to spread on a scone...or a set of silk sheets. No wonder Dmitri wanted her to wear it.

Of course, he also might have been influenced by the fact that the garment just missed being a size too small. If the saleswoman hadn't assured Reggie that the designer intended a snug fit, she'd have tried on a larger size. As it was, she remembered the material fitting her almost as closely as her skin, where it covered her skin, anyway. The abbreviated bodice sat off the shoulder and drew the eye to her breasts while the hemline fought for an equal share of attention by falling somewhere just long of indecent exposure.

Carrying it with her to the full-length mirror on the door, Reggie held it up against her body, smoothing a hand across the luxurious cloth. She had to give the man credit; he had fabulous taste. Stripping out of her robe, she pulled on her bra and thigh high stockings before she gave in and pulled on the dress.

She sighed at the feel of the heavy velvet against her skin when she finally wrapped the gorgeous garment around her. She struggled for a minute with the zipper until it slid up its full height to just below her shoulder blades, and she surveyed the results in the full-length mirror.

"Damn. It's perfect."

* * * * *

At precisely six thirty-five, Reggie stepped through the door of Captain Jack's Nightclub and took a deep breath. Well, as deep as she could without tumbling out of the low cut dress and giving the inhabitants of the bar a better show than the strip club down the street. She felt the weight of appreciative male glances sliding over her, even though she normally remained oblivious to that kind of attention. Tonight, she felt it, and it felt fabulous.

She knew she looked better than she had in a long time, maybe better than she ever had. The dress presented her lush curves like an offering, pushing her generous breasts together and raising them until they looked in danger of spilling from the neckline. The snug fit accentuated the smallness of her waist and hugged the curve of her hip until all eyes were drawn by the contrast. Her skin seemed to glow against the crimson velvet and the auburn silk of her hair, which she'd allowed to tumble in unruly waves down her back. Her legs were encased in the sheer, black, thigh-highs whose tops just barely managed to stay hidden under her hem, and her dainty feet disappeared into a pair of black stiletto heels.

All in all, Reggie looked like sex on a stick, and she wasn't the only person in the bar who thought so. Too bad Dmitri wasn't early enough to see her grand entrance.

"Reggie! What are you doing here?"

She automatically turned at the sound of her name, but when she saw who had called it, she swore quietly and creatively. Missy and Corinne sat at one of the small, round tables near the edge of the bar, and they waved her over with enthusiasm. Of all the rotten luck!

"Girl, after those messages Ava left you, I thought you'd be avoiding all of us like the plague. But look at you!" Corinne pulled back and gave her friend a comprehensive going over. "You are hot!"

"Absolutely. What inspired you?" Missy's eyes widened. "Are you meeting the guy from last night again? Where is he? Can we meet him?"

Reggie shifted.

"Tell us every dirty little detail," Corinne demanded. "I never even got a look at the lucky man, but I heard a rumor he makes gorgeous sound like an insult."

Reggie struggled for some way to weasel out of answering questions and was preparing to yell, "Fire!" at the top of her lungs when a hand fell on her shoulder.

"Reggie, thanks so much for agreeing to meet me." All three women turned at the sound of Greg's voice. He ignored Reggie's friends and took her by the elbow. "I got us a quiet table by the wall where we can talk."

Reggie froze and wondered which higher power she could have offended enough to land her in this situation. *Of all the bars in all the clubs in all the world, my friends just had to walk into this one.* The situation achieved an extra level of ironic pain due to the fact that the women seated beside her hated Greg with a passion, even more than Reggie had ever been able to bring herself to hate him. It spoke for their loyalty, but not for a pleasant meeting.

"Oh, have you learned to keep it in your pants long enough to have conversations these days, Gregory?" Corinne smirked, not even attempting to hide her contempt.

"Gregory has always been good at talking, Corinne," Missy said. Around Greg, even sweet little Missy turned brittle and cutting. "It was telling the truth that he had a problem with."

Greg glared at Reggie's friends, but for once, he kept his mouth shut and didn't let them drag him into a fight. Instead, he focused on Reggie and gestured to a table at the back of the bar. "Shall we?"

Reggie risked a quick look at her friends and registered their "Lucy, you got some 'splainin' to do!"

expressions. They'd just have to wait until later, because she was not about to pass up the opportunity to have Gregory Martin groveling at her feet in a public place. There were some things to which a girl simply did *not* say "no."

She murmured her agreement, cast her friends an "I'll tell you later" glance, and let Greg guide her to their table. She kept her head high and her shoulders back and added an extra swing to her hips when their path through the crowd forced her to walk in front of him. Let the twit salivate, because he was never going to lay a finger on her again.

The funny thing was she didn't feel Greg's eyes on her. Instead she felt the almost tactile sensation of someone else's gaze. Reggie looked around, expecting to see Dmitri poised somewhere in the shadows. He wasn't there, but she still could have sworn his fingers slipped beneath her hair and caressed the back of her neck.

She brushed the sensation off as imagination, at least until she felt the distinct pressure of a hand pat her ass and squeeze the cheek affectionately. She jumped about eight inches and looked around, but no one was remotely close enough to have touched her. She scowled, and a shiver raced through her.

Gregory noticed her tremble when he pulled out her chair, and he frowned. "Are you cold?"

"Not at all," she said. She looked warily around her again before slipping into the chair and pulling her attention back to the man in front of her. She smiled coyly and fluttered her lashes at him. "In fact, it's kind of hot in here. Don't you agree?"

Greg frowned. "Actually, I think it's pretty comfortable. But I wouldn't be surprised if you were freezing in that thing."

That thing? She hadn't expected Greg to refer to the sexiest garment she'd ever worn as a thing. He should have been having a completely different reaction, one that involved a loss of fine muscle control. And maybe panting.

She saw no panting, but she did feel someone's breath stir her ear and a warm, rough tongue reach out to toy with her earlobe. She spun around so fast she almost fell off her chair.

Careful, dushka. *You would not want to injure yourself by being careless.*

Damn it, Dmitri, she fumed. *You can't just sneak up on people like that. It's rude!*

Oh, is it? he purred. *As rude as exciting your lover and then leaving him unfulfilled while you sleep off your orgasm?* She felt his hand slide up her thigh and force itself between her legs, cupping over her bare pussy, and yet the only man close enough to touch her was Gregory, who nervously shredded a cocktail napkin in his two, very visible, as in not touching her, hands. *Is it as rude as that, Regina?*

Dmitri, not now. She shifted, figuring if his hands weren't really there, they couldn't affect her unless she allowed it. She would just pretend she didn't feel a thing.

"Are you all right, Reg?" Greg frowned, looking at her oddly. "Maybe that thing you're wearing really is too tight."

"It's called a dress, Gregory, and it's hardly indecent." She ignored the way the imaginary fingers between her thighs had begun to twine through her pubic hair, and focused her attention on Greg. The tips of her fingers trailed along the top of the bodice, calling attention to the way it cupped her breasts and emphasized her generous curves. "Some men think I'm very sexy in it."

She left her hand at the level of her shoulder and brushed her fingers back and forth over her bare skin. The sensation felt pleasurably stimulating, but not as stimulating as the fingers that clamped around her nipples.

Misha! she thought, her eyes going wide while her thighs clamped around the hand that slid from her damp curls to the tightly furled petals of her cunt. *Not here!*

"Kinky would be a better word." Greg frowned, his voice yanking her mind away from Dmitri's phantom touch and back to reality. "I never thought you were into that exhibitionist kind of thing, Reg."

She heard Misha chuckle.

"And I didn't know you were into your secretary, especially not so literally," Reggie snapped, cursing her overactive imagination and her oversexed psychic lover. She swept another look around the room, sure Dmitri must be lurking somewhere close by, but she still couldn't see him.

Frowning, she turned and caught a waiter's eye (which wasn't hard, since it was glued to her chest) and pointed at the beer bottle on the next table. If this was how the evening was going to go, she damn well needed a drink, even if she turned into an alky. "I guess we both needed to learn a little more about the other."

I know many things about you, dushka. *Shall I list them?*

Reggie heard the silky menace in those words and made a last ditch effort to focus her attention on Gregory.

The slime ball didn't even have the grace to look uncomfortable at her comment. Instead, he shrugged and fumbled in his pocket for a cigarette. Reggie had always hated that he smoked, so it made her feel better he kept such a repulsive little habit. It made her feel superior. And less likely to do something stupid, like be nice to him.

I think I can guarantee that you will be too busy to pay much attention to that boy, Regina. Shall I demonstrate?

Before her mind could form a coherent reply, his fingers shifted from between her legs. She had time for one relieved exhalation of breath before her thighs were uncrossed and opened wide beneath the table and the phantom fingers were replaced with an equally invisible tongue.

Unseen teeth nibbled at her engorged clitoris, and Dmitri's voice rasped sensuously inside her mind. *You aren't thinking about him now, are you, Regina?*

Who?

Dmitri chuckled in her mind even as his tongue stroked avidly between her legs, slicking her juices along the length of her slit and greedily lapping up the excess.

Reggie's hands clamped on the edge of the table, and she gritted her teeth to keep her eyes from crossing. Only the sheer force of will and the fear of humiliating herself in public kept her from voicing the moans building steadily up in her throat.

"Well, the thing is, Reg," Greg continued, oblivious to the strain on her face and her white-knuckled grip on the edge of their table. "I feel...I've felt...ever since I left the apartment, I've felt like...like something was missing. Like I left part of me behind."

Reggie didn't hear a bloody word he said. Instead, she heard Dmitri's wicked voice whispering through her mind, telling her all the things he wanted to do to her body, with her body, inside her body. She heard the ragged sound of his breathing and the unsteady thud of her own heartbeat. And above it all, her mind heard the wet, hungry sound of Dmitri's tongue and lips slurping at her streaming cunt.

Misha! she pleaded. *You can't. Oh, God, you can't do this here!*

His tongue worked harder against her flesh, circling her clit and tugging on the throbbing nub. His teeth scraped her swollen labia, and she felt his fingers press against her opening, demanding surrender.

"It finally dawned on me," Gregory continued, "just the other day, that I had done something really stupid. In fact, I think I made the biggest mistake of my life."

The biggest mistake of Reggie's life had been taunting Dmitri. She knew that now, knew it in every tensed muscle in her body while she waged a desperate and silent war to keep her pleasure from showing on her face or in her voice. If she let her self-control slip even a little, she would be writhing on the floor and begging to be fucked until she ended up the victim of a gang rape or a brand new patient at Bellevue.

Misha, I can't! Don't do this, please.

She lowered her head, squeezing her eyes shut while his ghost fingers tunneled deep into her cunt, curling forward to rake hard against the tender spot at the front of her pussy. She continued until she broke down and begged. "Stop!"

Gregory completely misunderstood. He thought she could even remember his existence.

"No, wait. Let me finish." The blond man reached across the table and caught her hand in one of his and gave it a gentle squeeze. "Reggie, I need you…"

I need you more, dushka, Dmitri whispered. *I need you to come now. Come for me,* milka. *I want to see you.*

Yes! Ah, Misha! Reggie bowed her head, bit her cheek until it ached and fought to hold herself completely still while her body tensed with the force of her climax. She forced her face to stay down, because there was no way she would be able to control her blush or the look in her eyes. The experience aroused her beyond anything she'd ever experienced. Anyone who looked at her face would know what was happening to her.

Hush, milaya. *I will allow no one to see your pleasure. This is a sight reserved for my eyes alone. Do not worry. I will care for you always.*

She gained control of her breathing just in time to hear Gregory's last few words.

"…to give me my grandmother's ring back."

Her eyes snapped open. "What?"

She couldn't possibly have heard correctly. Too much sex had clearly fried her brain, but if she could focus on being furious at Gregory, she might not do something rash to Dmitri. Like diabolically plot and execute his murder.

"My grandmother's ring," Greg repeated, sounding impatient. "It's an heirloom. She meant for me to give it to my wife. I never should have given it to you after her funeral."

Reggie recoiled from him like he'd suddenly developed running sores all over his body. If only fate would be so kind. "And now you want it back? What the hell is that about?" Of all the ways to ruin a post coital glow, this had to be among the sleaziest. "Who the hell do you think you are?"

Greg looked at her like she was short a few screws. "Reg, it was Granny's ring. She wanted to pass it down to her kids and grandkids. Obviously, I'm not going to be having those with you. I think it's only right that you give it back to me."

He sounded almost like he was trying to be logical about the whole thing. Logical! If he wasn't careful, she would make it impossible for him to ever sire children. With anyone. She was just sick and tired of the whole male species. It made her more determined to watch them die.

"I'll give you something, all right, Greg Martin," she hissed through her clenched teeth. She jumped down from her stool, ignoring the unseen hands that tugged her hem back down into legal parameters, and planted her hands on her hips. "I'll give you *hell* for being the insensitive, immature jerk you are. I know what this is really about! It's that secretary, isn't it? Or it's some other vapid young thing who's buying your sweet talk and your lies just like I used to do. But you're so shallow that you don't even realize how tacky this is! You're such an asshole—"

"Why, because I've moved on?" His expression went from vulnerable and conciliatory to snarky in less time than it took her to grit her teeth. "That's why you're really being such a raving bitch about this, Reg. You're jealous because I've moved on and found a new relationship, and you can't even get a man when you're dressed like a two-bit street whore."

By this point people were starting to notice their argument—not that any of them had noticed her getting eaten out by a figment of her imagination a few minutes ago— but Reggie was too pissed off to care. Not to mention Greg wasn't diffusing her anger by trying to make her look like the pathetic one. Admittedly, at least half her anger should be directed at Dmitri, but he remained scarce and Greg stood there looking all too handy.

"You ought to know about whores, seeing how many of them you've screwed!" she snarled, taking a step forward until she had to tilt her head up to look at him. "I'll have you know half the men in this bar would kill to go home with me tonight, so don't tell me I can't get a man, Gregory Ansel Martin!"

"Especially not when your man might find such a comment insulting."

Chapter Nine

Dmitri slid his arm around Regina in a replay of the previous night at the Goth club and glared at the arrogant little man who stood in front of them. He could feel the heat of his woman's anger while she stood stiff and distant under his embrace, but first things first.

"I have heard much about you, Mr. Martin. None of it has been good." He had read of this insect of a man from Regina's mind. Her memories tempted him to lash out with something violent and permanent to teach the man a lesson, but he didn't want to waste the time. "In the future, I suggest you refrain from insulting Regina. In fact, I suggest you stay very far away from her indeed. Is that clear?"

He tapped just far enough into the blonde's mind to find his character as loathsome as he had anticipated. He also saw the fool consider standing up to him, an idea Dmitri ruthlessly squashed. Eyes narrowing, he reached a little deeper into Martin's mind and squeezed, creating pressure like a hand closing over the human's throat. From where Reggie stood, he knew he appeared still and controlled, but his message sank slowly into Martin's consciousness. The human eyed Dmitri with growing fear and horror.

"I asked if you understood me, Mr. Martin."

He rumbled out the question in a tone that sounded like a purr but felt like a threat. From the corner of his eye, he saw Regina shiver. Greg trembled too, but for an entirely different reason.

"Yeah. Sure. Whatever you say, man. I gotta go."

And with that eloquent parting riposte, the degenerate Gregory Martin turned tail and ran. Very far away, indeed.

Reggie watched his flight with a smile that spoke less of humor and more of bloodshed. Really gory bloodshed. Dmitri barely had time to brace himself before she turned that smile on him.

It looked more like a snarl.

"I have never been so furious in all my life," she hissed, stepping toward him until they stood toe to toe. She had to crane her head to look up at him, but she didn't even seem to notice. "What the *fuck* did you think you were doing? How dare you do that to me in a public place!"

Dmitri's eyes narrowed to mirror hers while he fought down his own fury.

He'd known of her plans the instant he woke, but once the initial flare of rage had passed, he'd laughed at her vengeful streak. Trust his Regina to take an opportunity any other woman would have forged into a reconciliation and use it to twist an unsuspecting man into a knot for her revenge.

What he didn't like was thinking she would deny the pleasure he had given her and the knot she'd tied him into earlier that evening with her little show in front of her bedroom mirror.

He'd been barely awake, savoring the first glimmering return of consciousness when her image hit him. He'd known she found his note, had seen her in her bedroom thinking about the dress he'd told her to wear and about her date with Martin. His initial anger had barely faded when he teased her with silly comments and empty threats. He had never suspected what she would do to him.

He left when she ordered it and had drifted content in the dream-like world between sleeping and waking when she tugged at the path between their minds. He remembered his pleasure at knowing she had sought him out. The feeling had lasted only until she stripped of her clothes and proceeded to drive him out of his mind.

Even now, hours later, his body still throbbed at the memory. His cock had been hard since his rising, and she had the nerve to chastise him for arousing her by fulfilling yet another of her secret fantasies?

"I would not cast stones if I were you, Regina," he growled, his eyes sparking at her, his jaw set. "You should be grateful I allowed you to come. Or perhaps you would have preferred I left you hungry and aching for *four hours* while I arranged rendezvous with other women."

He grabbed her hand in his and forced her palm hard against his groin. His erection throbbed against the tight denim that covered him. "Would you have liked that, Regina?" he growled. "Would you?"

She looked into his eyes, and she must have seen something there that frightened her, because some of the fury leeched from her expression, and she softened. Her hand gentled and molded to his cock, cupping his thick length through the fabric.

"No, I don't suppose I would have," she admitted, her voice gentling just a bit. Before he could take her admission for surrender, she tightened her grip until her hand on his cock became as much a threat as a promise. "But I still don't think that's an excuse for what you did to me." Her gaze locked with his, and the serious tone of her voice matched her expression. "I'm not into public sex, Misha. I'd prefer it if what we share could remain private from now on. Understand?"

Dmitri nodded gravely. His Regina had strength and courage. It made him admire her all the more. "I understand, *dushka*."

"Good." Her lips softened into a smile, and her eyes glinted with humor. "Now I can tell you how cool it was to watch whatever you did to Greg. I haven't been that entertained in forever."

Dmitri chuckled. He seemed to recall several moments last night when she had appeared to be very entertained indeed.

Reggie looked up at him, and her eyes narrowed. "Don't look at me like that, buster," she warned. "Just because we got one issue straightened out doesn't mean we haven't got some other serious things to talk about. I hope you're wide awake and planning to stay that way until I'm finished ripping you a new one."

"Calm yourself, *dushka*," he murmured, her angry and empty threats amusing him. His little kitten could be so fierce. "We will talk as much as you wish, but I'm sure you would prefer to do so in privacy. Am I wrong?"

Reggie growled.

"I thought not. Come." He wrapped his arm around her and turned her toward the door, but they didn't get any farther.

"Well, well, what have we here?"

The interruption came from Ava, a figure he'd seen much of when he sifted through his Regina's thoughts. She stood before them, blocking their path to the door.

"Reggie, darling, aren't you going to introduce me to your new friend?" Ava's voice, low and melodic, and her expression, a sweet, warm smile, gave Reggie the creeps. Dmitri could read his lover's unease in her mind and her body.

"Um, sure," she muttered. Dmitri followed her glare to her friends from the club last night and the cell phone that sat on the bar table between them.

Stool pigeons, he heard Reggie think.

"Ava, this is Dmitri Vidâme. Dmitri, this is my friend Ava Markham."

"A pleasure," Dmitri murmured, taking Ava's hand in his and bowing slightly over it. The dark-haired woman's eyes narrowed at the gesture.

"I'm sure it is," she said, her tone dismissive. "It appears you've made quite an impression on our friend, considering you met her for the first time last night."

Dmitri's mouth quirked. Even without reading her mind, he could sense the protectiveness that radiated off Ava's slim frame. Reggie's friend had cool, faintly exotic dark looks that radiated confidence, sex and money. She stood close to five-ten in her Italian heels, and he knew her black sheath dress would bear an exclusive designer label. Ava was the sort of woman Dmitri would have been attracted to in the past, strong and aggressive and passionate, but Dmitri had recently discovered a decided preference for soft, cuddly redheads with submissive streaks.

"I am the one who was impressed, Ms. Markham. I am sure you realize your friend is a remarkable woman."

Reggie stepped forward as if to remind them of her presence.

"And she has a brain cell or two to rub together, not to mention a tongue in her head," she snapped, glaring at the two of them. "What is wrong with you people?"

"Nothing's wrong, Reggie," Ava said, pursing her lips and raising her chin. "I was simply curious to meet the man you met at the club last night. It's not like you to pick up strangers. You usually have better sense."

Dmitri stifled a chuckle. "I've found Regina has perfect sense. As well as many other…intriguing qualities."

Unable to resist, he settled his hand low and far back on Reggie's hip and squeezed, just for the entertainment value of Ava's reaction. She didn't disappoint him.

"She used to have perfect sense," Ava bit out, her dark eyes frosting over while she glared at Dmitri's hand. "But I'm seeing precious little of it at the moment."

Dmitri felt Regina stiffen under his hand.

"What's that supposed to mean?" Regina demanded, crossing her arms over her chest and glaring at her friend.

"It means there is something seriously wrong with you, Reg." Ava matched her glare for glare.

Dmitri could read the concern beneath the angry attack, but he didn't think Regina cared about the motivation.

"There is nothing wrong with me, Ava. And even if there were, it would be none of your business. I'm a grown woman. I can take care of myself."

"Then prove it by not letting some cretin paw you in public like you're a piece of meat!"

Dmitri hadn't planned to come between the two women—he hadn't lived this long by doing something so stupid—but neither would he stand by and watch Ava insult his Regina. He stiffened at her words and touched her mind, looking for an entrance.

"Dmitri is not pawing me, but even if he were, what business is that of yours?" Regina countered. "Maybe I like being pawed! Maybe I don't care what you think about me or the men I date!"

Man, Dmitri corrected, sending the thought firmly into Reggie's mind, briefly dividing his attention between the two women. *You date only one man, Regina. Me.*

He saw Regina roll her eyes, and he bit back a grin, turning his attention once more to Ava. She had a surprisingly strong mind with some impressive natural shielding. He probed quickly for a weak spot, but it didn't take long for him to realize he couldn't just slip quietly into her mind in the middle of a public place. She required more force than that, which meant their best strategy might be to retreat.

Dmitri turned away from Ava and squeezed Regina's hip gently. "Perhaps we should leave, *dushka*," he murmured. "I do not believe your friend appreciates our company."

Regina sent a last glare at Ava and let Dmitri urge her toward the door. "Maybe you're right, Dmitri. We can leave if you're ready."

Ava nearly screamed. "And maybe you're out of your mind! Listen to yourself, will you? You sound like the sort of empty-headed twit you've always hated. You've known this man for twenty-four hours and already you're letting him control you as if you can't think for yourself! What is your problem?"

Regina ignored her friend and walked calmly toward the door without glancing back. Dmitri guided her with his hand on her hip, but he didn't quite have her self-control. Just before they stepped down from the bar area, he looked back over his shoulder at Ava. Very consciously, he let his mask of polite control slip and showed her a glimpse of the things he kept inside.

He didn't think she'd confront him again.

* * * * *

Reggie never did get around to lecturing Dmitri on his mental snooping or his dictatorial tendencies. Three minutes after they returned to her apartment he had her stripped, spread and draped face-down over the side of her mattress while he tortured her with teasing, shallow thrusts of his fingers into her wet heat. At that point, telling him she didn't like it when he tried to control her seemed a bit hypocritical. She almost hated herself for the way he could make her pant.

"Misha!" She gasped his name like a magic word and braced her hands against the bed, shoving her hips back against him. The hand that rested in the small of her back and held her in place pressed firmly to keep her still.

What do you want, dushka?

She heard his voice, no matter how hard she tried to block him out. She could surround her thoughts with mental barbed wire, but somehow Dmitri could cut right through it and never feel a scratch. Her defenses became meaningless around him, and the thought terrified her. What if Ava had been right? Could she just lie back and let Dmitri turn her into a mindless little sex toy?

He pulled his hand free of her clinging heat, and she whimpered.

Tell me, milaya. *I want to hear you tell me.*

He wanted to make her beg, and part of Reggie screamed in protest, but the demanding flesh between her legs drowned out the rebellion.

"You, Misha. I want you."

Her whisper became a shocked hiss and then a moan of pleasure when Dmitri rewarded her confession with the hot stroke of his tongue between her thighs. She trembled and had to lock her knees to keep herself upright. Dmitri had slipped to kneel behind her, and he clamped his hands on her hips, pinning them firmly to the bed while he drove her slowly out of her mind.

You taste so sweet, dushka. *Sweet and spicy and delicious.*

It felt a thousand times more intense than his phantom touch at the bar, and it almost killed her to hear him speaking in his black magic voice while his tongue lapped wantonly at her pussy and drew tight little circles around her clit. Her breath came in helpless pants. She arched her back uncontrollably, tilting her hips to give him better access to her aching flesh.

That's right. Such a good girl. He crooned to her, his hands slipping from her hips to her thighs, gripping them and forcing them wider apart. His tongue pressed her more firmly, and he kept his hands clamped just above her knees, holding her open as securely as a spreader bar.

Reggie pressed her forehead to the mattress and squeezed her eyes shut. She wanted to get closer, wanted to get away. His mouth fed at her, drank her sweetness and pressed her faster and faster toward her climax. He seemed to sense exactly the moment when his teasing licks became unbearable, and his tongue pressed harder against her. He nuzzled lower and found her clit. Greeting the swollen nub with quick flick of his tongue, he drew it gently between his teeth and suckled. The sensation robbed her of the ability to reason, the ability to stand. Her body went limp and trembled. Dmitri gripped her legs and braced his shoulders against the back of her knees, pinning her upright against the bed.

She tried to beg him to fuck her, to come inside her and ride her hard, but she couldn't speak. All she could do was moan and gasp and pray for mercy. He gave her none.

He nipped lightly at her clit, sending a bolt of pleasure-pain coursing through her. She screamed, the sound little more than a shrill exhalation of air.

Tell me, dushka.

She couldn't speak, could barely think, but Dmitri would hear her. *I need you to fuck me. Please fuck me, Misha!*

He nipped her again, soothed the sting with his clever tongue. *No. Tell me who you belong to. Tell me you are mine. Tell me no other man will touch you.*

Yes! God, yes! No one else. I'm yours. I belong to you, Misha!

Dmitri growled his satisfaction and thrust three, long fingers deep into her grasping cunt. It was all Reggie needed.

She came, her entire body clenched and trembling. Her back arched, and her hips pressed high against him and her mind went blank and empty. She knew nothing but Dmitri and the pleasure that coursed through her. She didn't even know the sharp sting of his fangs or his harsh growl of pleasure when her blood mingled with her juices and slid sweetly down his throat.

Chapter Ten

Reggie woke the next morning already brooding.

Dmitri had kept her way too busy last night for her to think about the things Ava had said at the bar, but she remembered them now. In fact, they were the first thoughts in her head when her eyes opened and squinted against the late morning sunshine. When he wasn't there to cloud her thoughts with lust, Reggie could admit she did seem to act differently around Dmitri. Somehow he brought things out of her she'd been trying really hard to pretend weren't inside her to begin with.

Reggie considered herself a strong, independent women. She supported herself, thought for herself, acted for herself. She believed women should have the same rights and opportunities as men and should never allow themselves to be treated as if they didn't. If pressed, she would have called herself a modern feminist, a woman who appreciated men, but didn't need them to complete her or guide her or tell her what to do.

So why did it feel so good when Dmitri took control? It freaked her out that his assumption of command and dictatorial tendencies made her feel so safe and cherished. She should be railing against his attitude, not sighing with contentment when he took charge and arranged her and her life to suit him. When she felt his body against hers, it all made perfect sense, but now, in the bright light of day, she had to think Ava might have a point. Maybe she should be suspicious of Dmitri's autocratic personality.

She mulled it over while she dragged herself out of bed and pulled on her bathrobe. Once again, her muscles ached in a graphic reminder of the previous night, though this time she could add lack of sleep to her problem. Not only had Dmitri's demanding appetite kept her up way past her bedtime, but once he had let her sleep, she'd drifted into some really disturbing dreams.

She'd imagined they were back at the Mausoleum, only this time they danced together, completely naked on the crowded dance floor. The dream had been so real she'd felt the texture of his skin against hers, the cool surface of the wooden floor beneath her feet.

In her dream he surrounded and overwhelmed her, a lot like he did in real life. They had swayed to a slow, hypnotic rhythm, while the people around them continued to mosh to the frantic, industrial music she couldn't hear. They had ignored everyone else, totally wrapped up in each other while they danced. But the dancing had changed, and in the metamorphic way of dreams, in the next instant he had been pressing inside her.

They made love there on the dance floor. She'd felt Misha's hands slide down to cup her ass and lift her, and she'd wrapped her legs around his waist and lowered herself onto his waiting cock.

No one in the dream paid any attention while Reggie and Dmitri made love in their midst. The club patrons had swirled around the couple in a sea of heat and color, but all Reggie had really been able to focus on had been Misha's deep, black eyes. She'd stared into them while he thrust in and out of her until she'd gotten dizzy and hot and trembled on the edge of orgasm. In her dream, she'd continued to stare until he opened his mouth, and she could see his canine teeth elongate and sharpen until they'd become fangs. When he lowered his head and sank his teeth into her throat, the hot, piercing pain had tumbled her over the edge, and she'd come, her cunt greedily drinking his semen while his mouth greedily consumed her blood.

The dream had faded slowly, just like the orgasm, but the images lingered with her all night. Even after she woke, she could still feel his mouth drawing at her throat and his teeth holding her in place while he fed.

That's what she got for going to Goth clubs and fantasizing about vampires, she scolded herself, heading into the kitchen for breakfast. A shrink would probably love a transcript of that dream, but Reggie chalked it up to a late night, exhausting sex and the lingering tension from her confrontation with Ava. Apparently her subconscious thought there might be some truth to her friend's accusation that Dmitri's control of her might be unhealthy instead of just unbelievable.

She popped a bagel into the toaster and was measuring grounds into the coffeemaker when someone banged vigorously on her front door. Frowning, she slid the automatic drip basket into place, pushed the button and crossed to the door. Checking the peephole, she sighed and leaned her forehead against the cool wood. The Inquisition had arrived.

She opened the door and stepped aside to let her friends into the living room. She was on her way to the bedroom before the door closed behind them. "Coffee is on, and there are bagels in the freezer. If I'm getting the third degree, I'm damned well not going to do it naked."

"But I'm betting you ended up naked last night!" Danice's quip and the sound of laughter followed her all the way down the hall.

When she reemerged from the bedroom, still barefoot, but now dressed in worn jeans and a red knit top, her apartment smelled like a Jewish deli and sounded like a Chippendale's review.

Her friends had nixed the tiny kitchen and spread out coffee, fruit and bagels on her coffee table. Someone had dug out butter, cream cheese and two flavors of jam, and Missy was just setting down a skillet full of scrambled eggs when she looked up and caught sight of Reggie. "Somebody looks well-exercised." She grinned.

Corinne placed a serving of eggs on a plate, added half the bagel Reggie had toasted and handed it to her. "Sit. Eat. Talk."

"With my mouth full?"

"Don't be smart with us, Miss Thang," Danice warned. "You have a story to tell us and we are not going away until we hear it."

Reggie wasn't sure she wanted to talk about Dmitri right now. Heaving a theatrical sigh, she took a seat in an armchair and balanced the plate on her lap. "Once upon a time—"

She ducked just before a slice of orange would have bounced off her forehead.

"Try again, Reg. And this time skip straight to the hot monkey sex."

Corinne's order defeated the smart-ass strategy, but Reggie didn't want to share the details of the previous two nights with her friends, especially not with Ava. No matter how close they all were, she couldn't feel comfortable with painting them a picture of the most erotic experiences of her life.

And she still didn't want to open up the discussion with Ava about her actions around Dmitri. Instead of answering, she shrugged and pushed the eggs around on her plate. "That's pretty much it. We had hot monkey sex. He went home."

A chorus of groans and grumbles echoed through the apartment.

"A less than rousing tale." Ava leaned against the arm of her chair, directly opposite Reggie's, and cradled a coffee mug in her manicured hands. "We've all spoken about seeing you and your Dmitri together the last two days. I believe we were looking for a bit more detail about your...relationship, Regina dear—names, positions, dimensions."

Did two nights of amazing sex equal a relationship?

The others laughed, and Reggie blushed as red as her shirt, but she still managed a respectably convincing scowl. "If you want details, call a nine-hundred number."

"Why should we do that when we have you right here? For free, rather than five-ninety-nine a minute."

"But I'm not here to satisfy your prurient interests."

"Of course you are." Ava sipped her coffee and eyed Reggie over the rim. Her gaze locked on the side of Reggie's neck, and her eyes narrowed. "What's that on your neck, Regina?"

"What's what?"

Reggie's hand went reflexively to the spot that captured Ava's interest, but she didn't feel anything.

"Well, that's what I call evidence." Danice wanted to see and jumped up to brush Reggie's hand away. She stared at her friend's neck so long and so intently that Corinne laughed.

"What are you looking for?"

"Fang marks," Danice answered, grinning. "I wanted to see if Reggie maybe landed herself a real vampire."

Reggie blushed when she remembered her dream. "Don't be a jerk," she muttered, pushing her friend away.

"Looks like a garden variety hickey to me," Missy said. "Not exactly sophisticated, but I'm sure it added to the moment. Right, Reg?"

Reggie shifted uncomfortably and clamped her hand over the bruise. She'd noticed the mark yesterday morning when she dressed, which was odd, because she couldn't remember when Dmitri had marked her. She still might have to tell him to lay off the vampire act, especially after her dream. "Well, that's why we went there, right? I was supposed to get a Fix with a vampire-type guy. I did, and it's done. Who's up next?"

"Not so fast, Reg," Danice said, raising an eyebrow and crossing her arms over her chest. "You aren't getting off that easy. Part of the Fix is sharing the news with your friends, and providing a full evaluation. We still want details."

"I don't think Regina has to tell us anything she doesn't want to," Ava broke in. She surprised Reggie with her defense, but at that point, Reggie would have been glad for help from Genghis Khan and the Mongol hoards.

"Thanks, A —"

"Because I don't think Reggie's adventure counts as her Fix. She still needs to take care of that."

Reggie went pale. "What? But you can't Fix me. I mean, I already had a Fix. I mean, Dmitri was —"

"Not part of the game," Ava declared. "I had someone set up to take care of the two fixes you submitted, Regina, but you didn't stick around to meet him. Therefore, you missed your Fix."

"I didn't miss anything! Dmitri and I—"

"I don't care if your new friend wore a black cape, plastic fangs and made you call him 'master.' He wasn't your Fix, so he doesn't count."

Reggie's shirt paled beside her flaming cheeks.

"Oh, my God! He did!" Danice shot to her feet and did a little victory dance in front of the sofa. "Reggie's man fulfilled both her fantasies, and we didn't even get involved. You go, girl!"

Her appetite gone, Reggie set her plate down on the table and checked to see if there was room under it for her to hide.

"Wow, Reg. That is so cool! None of us were able to get our fantasies without a little help. And here you go and blow us out of the water." Missy grinned and gave her a thumbs-up sign. "I guess you didn't need our help after all."

"Let's not be hasty, Melissa." Ava set aside her empty cup. "Reggie may have gotten a couple of her fantasies fulfilled, but it wasn't an official Fix. We've all had dates outside of the Fixes, and it doesn't matter what happens on them. It's only the arranged Fixes that count. After all, we can't check with Dmitri, so how do we know Reggie isn't lying about the S&M just to get us off her back?"

Reggie saw the others taking Ava seriously and tried to cut in, but the other woman bulldozed right over her.

"I won't say it's impossible Reggie could be telling the truth," Ava continued, "but we have no way to know for sure. So I move we throw out these fantasies and start over. Reggie gets an all new Fix."

Reggie stared at her, astounded and terrified. "Oh, no!"

"You know, Ava may be right," Danice agreed, grinning. "Must be your lucky day, girl, because you're up again."

"Right. Can't have you missing another turn," Corinne said.

"Look, guys," Reggie began, trying to reason with them, even while the idea of sex with any man other than Dmitri made her stomach churn. "I appreciate what you're trying to do here, but it's really not necessary. Dmitri would—"

"Dmitri would what?" Ava asked, her voice soft but far from gentle. "You said Dmitri didn't control you, Regina. Was that true?"

"Yes, but I'm...involved with him. I can't do this. Ava, you said it yourself last week. I'm monogamous. Now that I'm involved, I can't just sleep with someone else."

Ava looked determined. "Two fucks do not make an involvement, Reggie. I don't care how good this guy was in bed. Unless you ended your date in Vegas in front of a JP, you're *not* exclusively involved. You never even said when you're seeing him again."

Reggie scowled. On the one hand she wanted to deck Ava, but there was the corner of unease inside of her that wondered if maybe her friend was right. Maybe she was letting Dmitri control her. Maybe she should strike a blow for independence while she still could.

She ignored the way her insides recoiled at the idea.

"Fine," she snapped. "Give me some paper, and I'll give you a new batch of fantasies."

"Oh, no." Ava's eyes glinted. "After last time, I don't trust you. I had Missy bring along your original fantasies. We'll draw from those."

Reggie stared at the papers in Ava's hand for a minute, then glanced up at her friends. They watched her expectantly.

"I still think—"

"Don't think, Regina. Just sit there and be a good girl while we Fix you."

Reggie let her head fall against the chair back, and she squeezed her eyes shut. After Dmitri, she wasn't sure any of her old fantasies still applied. It felt as if he'd fulfilled them all.

God, I'm like an addict, she thought, frightened by how deeply Dmitri affected her. *I think I might really need to do this. I've never acted this way about a man in my life. And I don't even really know him…*

"My, my, but you are an adventurous girl, Regina McNeill." Reggie heard the satisfaction in Ava's voice and decided she didn't want to know what had been drawn. "I'm sure that a very lucky man I know is going to love your night out together. In fact, I think both of you might come to view the opera in a whole new light."

The memory of that fantasy flooded her mind with erotic imagery, and Reggie buried her face in her hands with a groan. Every single image in her head painted Dmitri as that very lucky man. Too bad she'd be acting out the fantasy with someone else.

Chapter Eleven

For the first time in her life, Reggie experienced Monday morning with a sense of profound gratitude and relief. She could hardly wait to get to her office and discover the deluge of paperwork and crises that awaited her. At least maybe then she'd be able to think about something other than Dmitri and the stupid Fantasy Fix.

As it turned out, she wasn't. Oh, she had a hell of a day. The small ad agency where she worked had gotten word on Friday that they'd landed a major new account with an up and coming electronic retailer, and on Monday morning, Reggie found out she'd been assigned to manage their first project, putting together a new logo and corporate look. The sales and management team were high on the success, and the art department was reeling under their impossible new deadline. That left Reggie to smooth all the ruffled feathers and coax a miracle out of her design team.

But even while she fielded phone calls, reviewed meeting notes, composed emails and even talked a temperamental graphic artist out of quitting on the spot, her mind kept straying back to Dmitri. She felt a little like a new junkie who'd only just discovered her high and couldn't get the memory of it out of her mind. Only, in Reggie's case, the memories were also in her mouth, on her skin and hovering in the air around her.

She had barely slept last night, too caught up in her discovery that Dmitri's scent had lingered in her bed. She wrapped herself up in the sheets that bore his distinctive, intoxicating fragrance and wrapped her arms around the pillow he'd lain on. Her pussy had throbbed and ached and felt empty after two nights of erotic excess, but she hadn't wanted to chance Dmitri watching her again while she made herself come. She'd had to lace her fingers together around the pillow she held to keep them from straying between her legs.

In any other situation, she would have been embarrassed by her obsession, but she hadn't been able to help herself. She'd felt she would go crazy if she couldn't have at least the scent and the memory of him to wrap around her. She'd fallen asleep with the echo of his hands stroking against her skin.

And she'd woken up terrified.

She'd never in her life acted like this with a man. Even in her few and failed relationships, she'd seen her lovers as partners, as men she would share her life with. They had complimented her, but she'd been complete without them. With Dmitri, his absence from her life, even for one night, had been hell. She'd missed him like an amputated limb, with the same ache and disbelief and the phantom feel of his presence. She needed him, and the thought scared the crap out of her.

"Yoohoo! Earth to Regina."

Reggie snapped back to reality with an audible pop and tuned into Sherry's voice while the other woman tried to get her attention. "Sorry, Sher. What's up?"

The administrative assistant, whom Reggie shared with the two other Project Managers, rolled her eyes. "I hope you had a nice mental vacation there, because Banks is saying he needs to see the Alien Entertainment annual report draft five minutes ago."

Reggie sighed, pushed her chair over to the metal filing cabinet beside her desk and pulled out the appropriate folder. Charles Banks always wanted something five minutes ago, but since he owned the agency, she figured she could humor him.

"Here." She handed the thick folder to Sherry. "Tell him the photography is in the lab as we speak. Mike promised we'd have it by three."

"Cool. Thanks." Sherry turned to leave, remembered something and paused in the doorway. "Oh, I almost forgot. You've got a call on line four. Some guy."

"What does he want?" The last thing Reggie needed to deal with was an unknown artist hawking his talents.

"I asked, but he said it was personal business."

Dmitri.

For one, fabulous moment, the idea made her heart race and her stomach jump. Then reality set in, and she realized he had no way of knowing where she worked and so no way of getting her number. Giving disappointment and relief a chance to slow down her pulse, she took a deep breath and prepared her standard, "send us a portfolio and we'll get back to you" speech.

"Hello? This is Regina."

"Hi, Regina. This is Marc Abrahms. Ava Markham gave me your number."

Yikes, he must be the Fix. "Oh. Um, hi."

"Listen, I know you're at work, so I won't keep you," he said. *Well, he gets some points for manners, at least.* "But Ava mentioned you're an opera fan, and I was able to wrangle a private box for *Turandot* on Thursday night. I hoped you might join me."

Join you; fuck you. Why quibble over semantics? At least he was being delicate about the whole thing, even if that didn't keep Reggie's face from turning a peculiar shade of magenta. He could have just gotten right down to the bottom line and asked how many condoms to bring. "Um, well..."

"Ava's told me a lot about you," he offered in his pleasant, mellow voice. *Yeah, like the fact that I'm a guaranteed score.* "I'm really looking forward to meeting you in person."

I'll bet. His comment only made her blush harder, but there really was no graceful way out of the situation. Tightening her grip on the receiver, Reggie took a deep breath and said, "Sure. Thursday sounds fine."

"Great." He actually did sound happy that she'd accepted. *After what Ava must have told him, did he think I had a choice?* "If I pick you up at six, we can have dinner before the show. Does that sound all right?"

Reggie nodded, realized he couldn't see her, and hastened to reassure him. "That's perfect. I'll look forward to it." *Like a root canal.*

"Me, too. It was nice talking to you, Regina. Take care."

Reggie hung up the phone with a knot the size of Brooklyn twisting her stomach. The last thing she wanted was to spend Thursday night with a stranger, but she needed to exert her independence, to show herself she didn't need Dmitri, no matter how her mind and heart and body screamed for him.

She wasn't altogether sure she could bring herself to act out the opera fantasy with this Marc person. In fact, the more she thought about it, the more the idea made her uncomfortable. Her skin almost crawled, and the hair on the back of her neck stood on end. If she hadn't known her office was private and empty save for herself, she would have looked around to see if she were being watched. Her unease was that strong.

Shifting in her chair, she suppressed the urge to look over her shoulder anyway and neatly penciled the date with Marc onto her desktop calendar. As if she were likely to forget it.

She waited for her discomfort to ease, but if anything, writing down the date only made her illogical sense of foreboding worse. Reasoning with herself didn't seem to help, since even her conscious mind couldn't quite shake the idea that seeing any man other than Dmitri counted as some sort of betrayal, as if she were cheating on him.

"Ugh! Don't be ridiculous," she muttered to herself, tossing down her pencil and reaching for the stack of ad proofs she had to review. "I didn't promise Dmitri a damned thing, and he didn't even have the decency to call after he disappeared in the middle of the night again. This is not cheating. Get rational, Reg."

But there was nothing rational about the feeling telling her that although her speech might be logical, it was also very, very wrong.

* * * * *

The taste of her haunted him. If he could have dreamed of it he would have, but instead he staved off sleep as long as possible in order to preserve her flavor on his tongue. Dmitri knew he would never have enough of her.

He had dragged himself from her bed that second night, his head spinning and his cock aching. She intoxicated him, and he knew he would never be able to let her go. Regina was his mate, the one woman he could spend an eternity with and never grow bored.

The knowledge astounded him and echoed through him when he slipped into his rest just before dawn. She filled his last thoughts until he slept, and her image appeared to him the instant he fought back to awareness. His Regina. His woman. His mate.

He thought of her when he left his bed and made his way downstairs to his study. Not going to her immediately became an exercise in discipline. His fangs and his cock stretched and hardened at the thought of her, but he'd spent most of the weekend wrapped up in her, and even vampires had work to do. Besides, if he cleared off his desk tonight, Regina would have time to recover from his demands of the last two nights and would be rested and ready for him again soon.

Settling behind his desk, he logged on to his computer and got down to business. Over the course of his long life, he had developed a talent for financial matters, and with little else to occupy him through the years, he began to look on business as a game. Like chess, it all boiled down to strategy and to warfare, two concepts with which Dmitri felt very comfortable. He substituted corporations and mergers for pawns and checks and moved everything along according to his plans and to his whims. It had made him an extremely wealthy man.

Tonight he used business as a distraction. It kept him from butting yet again into Regina's mind, a habit he knew she hated, but which gave him so much pleasure. He adored listening to her thoughts, appreciated her sharp sense of humor and the overwhelming core of honor and love underlying everything about her. She fascinated him.

Before he could sink completely into thoughts of her, his phone rang.

"Vidâme," he answered automatically.

"So, you didn't wind up breathing wood this weekend. I started to wonder."

"Good of you to be concerned. I'm sure that's why you called."

Graham laughed. "Well, I did want to ask if your snack was as tasty as she looked, but somehow I don't think you're going to tell me."

"Lupines *are* renowned for their acute instincts…"

"That's what I thought," the werewolf chuckled. "I'm assuming you spent last night with your little hors d'oeuvres since I didn't see you at the club."

Graham owned a private club on the Upper East Side called Vircolac. Dmitri had been a member for longer than Graham had been alive, but then, the club had been founded in the eighteenth century. Graham had acquired it the old-fashioned way. He'd inherited it.

"Why is it that you persist in referring to humans as menu items?" Dmitri asked, ignoring his friend's unspoken question. "It's a little creepy."

"Creepy? You're the one who uses them for food, and I get called creepy?"

"And you use them for entertainment. Does that mean I should refer to them as tennis balls when I'm speaking to you? Or do you prefer Frisbees?"

"Touché. Clearly your *lady friend* made an impression on you."

"She is my mate."

Silence.

"Have you told anyone?" Graham sounded cautious and slightly stunned.

"No. There hasn't been time."

"Yeah, I can see that." He paused again, and Dmitri could hear when the thought occurred to him. "Have you told her?"

Dmitri laughed. "I'm surprised you thought to ask."

"Well, humans tend to have…interesting reactions to the whole vampire thing, let alone to a proposal of marriage from one. Most of them don't know a thing about you guys. How did she take it?"

This time Dmitri paused. "I don't know yet."

"Then you haven't told her. Which means you haven't turned her, either."

"No. And I'm not planning to do it unless she asks."

"Ohhh-kay, if you say so." Skepticism laced the werewolf's voice. "Can I buy a ticket to be there when you break the news?"

"Smartass. You should be careful around me, or I will have to sic her friends on you."

Graham scoffed. "What? Will those nasty human women kick me in the shins or something?"

Dmitri grinned and told his friend the story of the Fantasy Fix. The information he'd gleaned from Regina's mind still managed to amaze him. He'd never known human women with imaginations quite that vivid. He described the basic nature of the club, how he and Regina had met, and paused for Graham's reaction.

"Wow. Her friends sound…entertaining. If I met a human female so adventurous, I might break my rule about dating them."

Dmitri's grin turned wicked. "I could set you up with one of them."

"Bite your tongue, fang. I was joking. I don't do humans."

But Dmitri did. He had done one extremely intriguing human several times the night before, and he could barely control his impatience to do her again.

After he hung up the phone, he forced his mind onto his work and quickly discovered the results of his inattention over the past couple of days. Any man who commanded an empire as large as that of Vidâme International could not afford to take unexpected vacations. He had a lot to do if he were going to catch up.

He worked all night and well into the morning. He paused a few times to stretch, but didn't bother to eat. The blood he had taken from Regina the night before sustained him longer than any ever had, and he savored the additional proof she was meant to be his mate. She could sustain him indefinitely, nourishing both body and soul.

Though his energy flagged a few hours after dawn, the time when he normally would have been fading into sleep, he worked until he had completed all his pressing business. He even did a little advance planning in order to free up more time to spend with Regina. Finally, just before midday, he set aside the last of his correspondence, gave into temptation, and reached out to her.

He kept his touch light this time, knowing his intrusion had angered her the other day. He slipped into the edge of her mind, keeping his presence veiled from her while he simply sat back and savored the contact. At least until he discovered what she'd been up to that morning.

With ruthless precision, Dmitri caught the edge of her memory and reviewed her conversation with her friends, as well as the phone call she'd taken at her office just an hour ago. When he discovered the result of those conversations, his expression hardened, and he removed himself from her mind, taking one last piece of information with him when he went.

Regina had agreed to a date with another man.

I will kill him, he decided. *I will kill him while she watches, and then I will throw his body to the jackals and lock her in the tower of the castle I will purchase on a remote island in the North Sea, and I will fuck her until she understands the consequences of dating other men.*

And as for Ms. Markham, he reflected grimly. *She is one woman who needs to be taught to mind her own business.*

* * * * *

Monday was a very good day for Ava. She'd stolen a very hot new model away from one of her competitors and signed him up to her agency. She'd negotiated a multi-million dollar deal with a notoriously stingy *parfumier* that her models would be the exclusive reps for his new ad campaign, and she'd heard from Marc Abrahms that Reggie had agreed to their date.

She had also found out some very interesting things about Regina's new friend. Like the fact that Dmitri Vidâme owned a billion-dollar corporation called Vidâme International that had its fingers in an awful lot of pies. Or that Vidâme had no family, even though his ancestors had supposedly lived in New York since the early eighteenth century. Every little thing she found out made her more suspicious about the man, and she was determined to uncover all his secrets before he could hurt her friend.

All in all, when Ava snuggled under her down duvet just after midnight, she felt remarkably content.

Dmitri almost hated to shatter her happy little illusions, but she meddled into affairs that were none of her concern. She needed to learn a lesson, and he would be the one to teach it.

He waited patiently until she drifted off to sleep — which didn't take very long after her fourteen-hour workday — and slipped casually into her subconscious.

In another time, her mind would have fascinated him. He'd observed at the bar the other night how much more Ava resembled the women he'd involved himself with in the past. Now he could see the truth of that mentally as well as physically. Regina's friend possessed a brilliant, creative mind and the iron-willed determination of a military dictator. No one had ever managed to dig up so much information on him in such a short period of time. Her acumen impressed even him, and he made a mental note to include her agency among his investments.

Still, while he sorted through her mind, the unfamiliar feel of her only deepened his hunger for Regina. This woman, as complex and beautiful as she might be, left him cold, while Regina set him on fire.

He hurried about his task, anxious to get it over with so he could focus his attention back on his new mate, who would still require a good amount of skill and finesse before she grew accustomed to the idea of being his.

When he slipped from Ava's thoughts thirty minutes later, he found himself exhausted. Tampering with the woman's mind had required more effort than he'd anticipated, and he felt he might not have been as thorough as he wanted, but he'd laid the groundwork. Ava Markham's suspicions of him had been set on the back burner, and she would find her business concerns took precedence over everything else in her life for at least the next few days. He figured that should give him enough time to secure things with Regina, and once she admitted her bond to him, he knew not even Ava could come between them. And just to be sure she stayed away until he had Reggie tamed, he would have Graham and his pack keep her under watch. The werewolves did a mean stakeout.

He slipped out of the apartment as silently as he had entered. He hoped now he could stay out of all but one mind, because he needed to conserve his strength for Thursday night, when Regina's date would deviate slightly from what she was expecting.

Slipping his cell phone from his coat pocket, he made the arrangements.

* * * * *

They writhed together on the Persian carpet, the flashes of skin like cream and cocoa in the flickering firelight. A fall of pale, blonde curls caressed a nipple the color of raspberry truffles. A hand, slim and dusky, slid between pale, silken thighs and disappeared in the rosy, wet cavern they concealed.

Natalie moaned, her mouth full of dark, puckered nipple, and reached up to brush her own slender fingers over her lover's pouting lips. Simone opened her mouth, drew the fingers deep and sucked, humming her pleasure.

With her free hand, Natalie reached out, felt across the soft, nubby fabric of the rug until her fingers closed around a cool column of sinuously curved glass. Her mouth curved into a wicked smile, drawing back from Simone's nipple to lave the ruched peak with the tip of her tongue. Pulling her fingers free of her lover's mouth, she positioned herself at the other woman's side so that her hips could rock against Simone's fucking fingers while she had free access to her friend's cunt.

Closing her teeth around one dark nipple, she grasped the other between finger and thumb and gently squeezed while she brought the glass dildo between Simone's thighs.

Simone shivered at the press of cold, slick glass against her heated cunt. Moaning, she drew two fingers free of Natalie's dripping core and a moment later speared her again with three. She twisted her wrist, screwing her hand deeper, even as she lifted her own hips in search of greater sensation.

Growling low in her throat, Natalie closed her teeth more tightly around Simone's nipple and increased the pressure of her fingers. She slid the dildo back and forth through her lover's slit, gathering moisture and slicking the smooth surface of the glass. The toy slowly warmed, taking on the heat of the woman's body as Natalie circled it around the engorged clit and teased it against the rim of the quivering vagina. Her expression revealed the extent of her excitement, how much she enjoyed toying with the responsive female flesh beneath her hands and mouth.

Simone's hips canted upward. "*Ah, Natalie!*" she moaned, her head thrashing against the carpet. "*Ma chere, baisse-moi!* Fuck me! Please!"

Natalie chuckled and lightened her touch, running the slick glass over Simone's swollen vulva, deliberately bypassing her clit and her grasping cunt.

"Bitch!" Simone hissed and twisted her body in a lithe, rapid motion until her nipple popped out of the other woman's mouth and her free hand clamped over Natalie's mound. She slid two fingers deep, catching the blonde's clit between them and scissoring them together until Natalie moaned. Simone grunted in satisfaction and finger-fucked the other woman with hard, rapid thrusts, her fingers curled to rub the g-spot with every pass.

Her head fell back to her shoulders, and Natalie thrust the dildo home, burying it deep in Simone's dripping cunt. Her knees buckled, and she fell to the floor beside the other woman. Their bodies tangled together, legs entwined, hands burrowing between sweat-dampened thighs. They came together, lips meeting, tongues thrusting, kissing until they might have devoured each other. Moans and whimpers broke from them and filled the room with the rough, desperate sounds of sex.

About that time, Graham realized he needed help. Two of the most beautiful women he'd ever seen writhed naked and horny on the floor in front of him, and all he could think about was heading home for a cold beer and a nap.

It was just sad.

He sat sprawled in a chair in front of the fire in Natalie's parlor watching two stunning women fuck each other silly, and his dick barely twitched. Any man who could be bored by that should get counseling.

When his cell phone rang, barely audible over the wet, sucking sounds of clinging cunts and the squeals of female pleasure, he reached for it like a lifeline.

"Yeah?"

"I am glad I reached you, *bratok*."

"That you did, brother," Graham answered. "What's up?"

A female voice rose in a wild cry that traveled clearly over the airwaves. Dmitri paused. "Did I call at a bad time?"

Graham scowled and stood, padding naked to the other side of the room and propping his shoulder against the fireplace mantle. "No, it's no problem. What's up?"

Dmitri accepted the statement easily. "I need you to do me a favor."

Graham hoped it was an urgent favor, one that needed immediate attention. "You got it. What do you need?"

"I need you to arrange for your pack to do some surveillance for me."

"Done. Who are we staking out and why?" *And do I need to start tonight?*

"It is a woman, a friend of my mate. She is something of a troublemaker, and she does not approve of me. I need to be sure she stays out of the way until I have things settled with Regina."

Graham crossed his ankles and ignored the increasing tempo of moans and curses from the other side of the room. He could smell the mingled fragrance of the women and the sex, but he ignored it. "So that's your paragon's name. I was starting to wonder if you were ever going to tell me."

Dmitri chuckled. "I will even allow you to meet her, once I have settled her down," he said. "Provided that you keep your hands to yourself."

Graham rolled his eyes. If he wasn't interested in fucking either or both of the exquisite female vampires who just then screamed out their mutual climax, he doubted a simple little human would send him into a lustful frenzy. "I don't think you need to worry. Why don't you tell me more about this job?"

Dmitri gave him the woman's name, Ava Markham, and her address. Graham was grateful Natalie and Simone had finished with each other and lapsed into silence. At least now he could hear. He didn't bother to take notes because he would remember every detail. Most people said Graham had a mind like a steel trap, but he preferred to compare it to a filing cabinet. Once he learned a piece of information, he stored it away in its proper place and when he needed it again, he knew exactly where to find it.

He listened to Dmitri give him the details and paid little attention when Natalie padded naked across the carpet and offered him his abandoned snifter of brandy. He waved it away without ever looking at her. Later, he realized that had been his big mistake. He stiffened, in more ways than one, when the blonde sank to her knees in front of him and took his cock between her crimson lips.

Her mouth, soft, warm and wet, closed around him. Even boredom couldn't keep him from hardening at the sensation of the steadily increasing suction, but he showed no other reaction. His breathing remained deep and steady, and his voice didn't change as he discussed logistics with his friend over the cell phone. He saw out of the corner of his eye when the blonde crooked a finger at Simone, and he frowned down at the second woman as she slid between his body and Natalie's.

There wasn't a lot of room there, but Simone used it to her best advantage. She lay down beneath his spread legs and wrapped her legs around Natalie's waist. Then she scooted forward and raised herself into a reclined sitting position and slid her moist, skillful tongue over the surface of his testicles.

He tensed briefly and frowned down at Natalie, since he couldn't see Simone's face. Natalie had a wicked gleam in her eyes and her mouth stuffed full of his hardening cock. When Simone opened wide and gently sucked one round sac into her mouth, he hardened completely. Natalie hummed her approval, and her head bobbed faster up and down his length.

"That's no problem," he assured Dmitri, grasping a handful of Natalie's hair and holding her still with his cock half in and half out of her talented mouth. He couldn't reach Simone. She continued to suck his testicles, alternating between them until both his balls felt cool and slick with her saliva. "How close an eye should we keep? Are we talking a twenty-four-seven thing?"

Graham listened while Dmitri explained, and Natalie drew back from him, pouting. He ignored her and spread his legs wider when Simone drew a slick trail behind his balls and teased her tongue against his perineum. Eyes narrowing in jealousy, Natalie reached for his discarded brandy glass and warmed the fragrant liquor between her palms. Then she painted the amber liquid over his testicles and leaned forward to taste him.

Natalie's quick, pink tongue lapped the brandy from around the base of his cock while Simone caught the drips from his scrotum. Their mouths brushed and the women engaged in a deep, heated kiss before turning their attention back to the man between them. Their arms crossed at his hips, Natalie reaching back to massage his firm buttocks while Simone slid her hands forward to grasp and milk his hard cock.

"Don't worry," he assured Dmitri, sliding his hands back into Natalie's hair, but this time cradling her closer to him. "I'll see to it myself, and I'll have someone on her by dawn."

A few short words later, he flipped his cell closed and set it on the mantelpiece, then reached down to grip a fistful of each woman's hair, tugging them to stand in front of him.

"You know, it's very rude to distract a man when he's on the phone," he said, running his gaze over them, taking in their tight, swollen nipples and moist, bruised lips.

Simone wrapped her arms around one of his biceps and pressed the length of her naked body against his. "And are you going to punish us for it, *cher*?"

Graham shook his head. "You'd enjoy that too much."

Natalie laughed, a low, husky, sexual sound, and pressed herself against his other side. "But so would you, *mon amour*. So how can we lose?"

Graham shook his head and reached down, sliding a hand between each woman's legs and slipping his fingers deep into two lush, dripping cunts. "But I'm not in the mood, Nat, so unless you two want to get yourselves off again, you'll just have to live with what I want."

Natalie hummed and circled his cock in one hand, her fingers barely closing around his girth, while Simone cupped his balls in her palm and massaged gently. The darker woman leaned forward and flicked her tongue against his flat nipple.

He thought about it for a moment, but despite his body's reflexive arousal to their deliberate stimulation, he didn't feel particularly inspired. He could almost sense his familiar boredom lurking in the background, waiting to spring.

"I want you to go fetch that dildo," he said, pointing at the abandoned toy on the other side of the room. "And you," he continued, turning to Simone, "I want on your hands and knees right here."

Both women hurried to obey, their eyes—one set a pale, ice blue, the other a rich, warm cocoa—flashing with lust.

When Natalie returned with the dildo, he took it from her and thrust it immediately between her legs. The glass had cooled after the women had finished with it, and Natalie reacted immediately to the cold, her cunt clenching hard around the invading glass as she cursed Graham.

He cut her off by the simple and expedient method of covering her mouth with his, and since her tongue met his eagerly, nearly sucking off his taste buds, he knew she was far from upset by his actions. He ate at her mouth, nipping her lips and tongue while she gasped and opened wider for him. He thrust the dildo higher and harder into her, and she moaned into his mouth.

He heard an echoing moan from near his feet and looked down. Simone knelt on all fours beside him, licking her lips, her eyes fastened on Natalie's weeping cunt. Graham wiped a rivulet of juice from the blonde's inner thigh and extended his hand to Simone. She sucked his fingers clean and purred her pleasure.

Abruptly, Graham pulled back from Natalie and gestured to the floor beside Simone. "Lie down," he ordered.

She obeyed instantly, squeezing her thighs together and dropping to her knees to make sure she didn't lose the dildo on the way down. She rolled to her ass and laid down, her eyes glued to Graham's rampant cock.

Simone reached out to pet the other woman's wet bush, and Graham nudged her foot to get her attention. "Straddle her left leg and press your knee against the dildo," he instructed. "It's your job to make sure it doesn't come out."

Natalie shuddered, her eyes drifting half-closed as Simone positioned herself. Graham took a moment to admire the sight of the dark, round limb pressed hard against slim, white thighs and dripping, blonde cunt before he grasped Simone's hips in his hands and positioned himself to kneel behind her.

"Now be polite and make sure you don't come before your playmate does," he growled just before he plunged his entire length deep into Simone's eager pussy.

The impact staggered her and forced her knee hard against Natalie, and both women screamed in savage pleasure. Graham grunted and leaned forward, pressing his weight against Simone's back and releasing her hips so he could grasp one of her dangling breasts in his right hand, his left extending forward to close around Natalie's turgid nipple. He massaged roughly but carefully as he thrust with blatant force into Simone's weeping core.

Her pussy clamped around him, hot and wet and eager as she slammed her hips back against his and braced her hands in the curve of Natalie's waist to hold the woman still. He could hear the sucking sound of Simone's cunt as he pounded into her and the moist echo of the dildo rocking back and forth in Natalie's willing body. Both women moaned and dripped their pleasure, their juices combining with the sweat of three frantic bodies to turn them into a slick, glistening pile of flesh.

Graham's hands closed hard, pinching each woman's nipple in a fierce grip as he reared back and braced himself to hammer harder, his pelvis slapping roughly against Simone's ass with every thrust. She squealed and bowed down, folding her body until her hips pushed high against Graham and her forehead rested between Natalie's breasts. The blonde's tits jiggled with every thrust as Graham's energy funneled through Simone to rock the woman beneath them.

Suddenly Simone's knees gave out, and she collapsed on top of Natalie, their bodies glued together with heat and sweat and cum. Graham barely missed a beat. He reached forward and lifted Simone's right leg until she straddled Natalie's thighs. Then he pressed his own knee hard against the blonde's cunt, braced his palms on the carpet and renewed his vigorous thrusts.

Natalie and Simone moaned in unison, their mouths fusing in a desperate kiss. Their tongues mated, lips sucked, hands grasped until they became like one body beneath Graham, and he draped himself over Simone's back, still careful to keep his weight from her, licking the sweat off the nape of her neck before burying his face in the curve of her shoulder.

The women broke apart, and Natalie turned her face to Graham's, begging for a kiss. He complied, but she pulled away quickly and nibbled along his jaw, ducking her head toward his throat. Graham saw the flash of fangs and reared back, forcing his hips forward until his cock butted hard against Simone's cervix. The woman whimpered.

"No way," he growled, scowling. "You know the rules, Nat. No biting when we fuck. If you two are hungry, you can wait until we're done." He pulled back until just the tip of his cock remained inside of Simone. "Unless you'd rather eat than screw."

"No!" Simone wailed, squirming in an attempt to take him deeper inside her. "She'll behave. We'll both behave, just don't stop, *cher*!"

Graham watched Natalie and butted his knee forward, sending the glass dildo deep against her womb. She came on a scream, bucking so hard she threatened to dislodge Simone. Graham grasped the other woman's hips and held her steady, pumping hard into her until she too came apart. He grunted in satisfaction and hurried toward his own orgasm. A few short thrusts later, he came, emptying himself in Simone's still quivering pussy and somehow still feeling unsatisfied.

As he pulled away and rolled to an unoccupied spot on the carpet, he decided he would take care of this stakeout himself. If he could screw himself silly in a threesome with two, beautiful, female vampires and still feel the persistent twinges of boredom, he definitely needed a change of pace.

That or a psychiatrist.

Chapter Twelve

Halfway though the appetizers, Reggie forced herself to admit that Marc Abrahms was a really nice guy. By the time their waiter at the swanky little French restaurant delivered their entrees, she'd even worked up a sense of regret that she couldn't make herself excited about the prospect of sleeping with him.

Smiling at him across their table, she half-listened to his story about his car breaking down in rural Alabama (which was genuinely amusing), and tried to figure out why she couldn't muster up even a flicker of attraction for Ava's friend. She knew Ava would want a full report, even though Reggie hadn't heard from the other woman since Sunday. Her calls had gone unanswered, and she had figured Ava just didn't want to hear any complaints.

Not that Reggie had any right to complain about having Marc as her Fantasy Fix. He was definitely good-looking. In fact, he was more her type than...than some other people she'd met recently. Blond streaks highlighted his light brown hair, but they looked like the kind that came from hours in the sun rather than hours in a stylist's chair. His skin was lightly tanned, confirming the impression that he didn't spend his life locked up at the office. His blue eyes sparkled with animation, and his face looked just lived-in enough to save him from being pretty. He was built like perfection, strong and fit without being muscle-bound. All in all, the man ranked up there at "yummy," but Reggie had to work to push away the thought that his eyes would be sexier if they were dark enough to look black in the dim restaurant lighting.

Stifling a sigh, she looked down at her plate and wondered if she could at least work up some enthusiasm for the braised pheasant with haricots and baby potatoes. So far, she hadn't had any luck.

"You're quiet. I guess my adventures with Dewayne and Bubba have lost their sparkling allure."

Startled, Reggie raised her head to find him watching her with a raised eyebrow and an expression of faint amusement. "I'm sorry. I've been really rude," she apologized. "You've been a lot of fun, but I guess my mind was someplace else."

And it really was unforgivable of her, especially since she hadn't heard from the source of her torment since Saturday. He didn't deserve her attention, and Marc didn't deserve her rudeness. Even if her enthusiasm for this date didn't threaten to boil over, Marc was a nice enough guy that she ought to be polite. Forcing her distracting thoughts from her mind, she traded her fork for her wine glass and smiled at him. "I'm back, I promise. No more mental vacations."

Marc returned her smile and gracefully changed the subject. "So why don't you fill in some of the blanks Ava left me with. Where are you from originally?"

Oh good, small talk. Reggie thought she could handle small talk.

"Why? Is my accent not New Yawk enough?" she teased. "I grew up in Connecticut."

"Ah, that explains it."

When he didn't elaborate, Reggie's curiosity overcame her. "Explains what?"

"You. You've got a little bit of princess in you. Must be that country club air you were born in."

Reggie couldn't get offended when his expression so clearly told her he was teasing. Still, she mocked outrage. "Country club! I'll have you know, not all of Connecticut is Greenwich or Cos Cob, thank you very much. Some of us Nutmeggers come from families that worked for a living. I certainly don't expect to be treated like a princess." She gave him a righteous look while she set down her wine glass and schooled her face into an exaggerated picture of haughty arrogance. "I think Queen of the Universe is more fitting, don't you?"

Marc chuckled. "Sorry, your majesty." He drained his one glass of wine, but waved the waiter away when he would have refilled it. When he focused back on Reggie, his expression looked more serious. "You know, when Ava told me about you, she said you were just out of a bad relationship, and she worried you didn't get out enough. But now that I've met you, and seen you in person, I have a hard time believing you're lacking for invitations. So it's got to be a lack of interest on your part."

Reggie took a second to adjust to his honesty and to digest what he was saying. "Well, it's not as if I have men beating down my door…"

"If you don't, it's not because they don't want to." She shook her head like she planned to protest, and he held up a hand. "I hope you're not going to play at being modest now. We both know you're beautiful."

He stated it so matter-of-factly that Reggie just blinked. "Thank you. But not every man out there shares your taste for women who look like me."

"Sexy?"

"Round."

"Wrong word." He shook his head and ran his gaze over her. "You are definitely not round. Curvy? Uh-huh. Lush? Yes. Mouthwatering? Absolutely. But not round."

"Certainly not round. And even more certainly not available."

Reggie almost jumped out of her seat when the voice that had been haunting her dreams all week sounded from just above her head. Whipping around, she saw Dmitri standing beside her chair with one arm resting on the back and his gaze fixed on Marc. His posture and attitude had become so familiar she spoke before she thought about it.

"Misha, you have *got* to stop doing that."

Dmitri flashed Reggie an amused glance. *I am pleased that you remember how to address me,* dushka, *but you should not contradict me in public.*

Reggie rolled her eyes and prepared to argue, feeling more energetic and alive than she had since Saturday night. So what if he was doing impossible things again, like talking to her in her head. She could deal with that, sort of.

She never got the chance to protest his interruption because Marc pushed back his chair and stood.

The two men eyed each other for a long, tense moment, one dark and mysterious and intense, the other fair and frank and just as intense. They took each other's measure, each evaluating the situation and the other man while the maitre d' hovered in the background, clearly unsure of what he ought to do and whether or not he could pull it off even if he decided.

Finally, Marc's mouth quirked in amusement, and he held out his hand. "Marc Abrahms. I take it you're a friend of Regina."

"Yes, a...close friend. Dmitri Vidâme." He shook Marc's hand politely, but his other hand moved from the back of Reggie's chair to the shoulder left bare by her strapless evening dress.

Marc acted as if he didn't catch the movement, but Reggie felt sure he noticed. Damn men. They could always read each other's shorthand.

"We were just about to have coffee," Mark remarked. "Would you care to join us?"

That was going a little too far. Reggie shook her head. "That's really not —"

"Thank you." Dmitri squeezed Reggie's shoulder to silence her. He only had to look back at a waiter, and a third chair appeared at the table. He sat.

Marc, too, resumed his seat, and the waiter poured three cups of coffee before beating a hasty retreat to the relative safety of the kitchen.

Reggie ignored the coffee, infinitely more interested in glaring at the two men. They ignored her *and* the coffee.

"So, where are you from, Dmitri?"

"I was born in Kiev, though I have lived in many places during my life. I have called New York home for many years now."

Christ, they were treating this like a cocktail party! Reggie glared at them both, but neither one was paying her any attention.

"And what is it that you do?" Marc asked, tempting Reggie to kick him under the table. He didn't even blink. He just shifted his legs out of her reach, making her wish she'd worn steel-tipped combat boots rather than sexy, strappy sandals.

"I have a variety of business interests," Dmitri hedged, "but currently my most absorbing interest is of a more personal nature."

Marc observed the look Dmitri gave Reggie, watched the silent exchange between them and sighed. "Yes, I imagine it is." He signaled to the waiter and quickly paid the bill. "It was very interesting to meet you, Dmitri; and Reggie, I had a wonderful time." He stood. "But I do have to run. You two enjoy your evening."

He grabbed his jacket, shrugging into it while Reggie shot to her feet.

"But what about the opera?" she asked, feeling awful about Dmitri's behavior.

Marc smiled, and when he spoke, his voice was wry. "I don't think the opera would work for us, Reggie. But I wouldn't want you to miss it. Why don't you and Dmitri go and enjoy yourselves?"

Reggie was still trying to wade through all the double entendres when Marc extended two tickets to Dmitri, who refused with a shake of his head.

"Thank you, but it is not necessary," Dmitri said. "I maintain a private box of my own. Regina and I will be using it tonight. You should keep your tickets."

"It's not like I'm going to use them," Marc sighed, but he slipped the tickets back into his jacket pocket. "I guess the box will just have to sit empty for the night. Now, if you two will excuse me, I'm going to go home, pour myself a nice big glass of bourbon and see if I can catch the last few minutes of the game."

He walked away before Reggie could protest again, so she turned to Dmitri, intending to take her embarrassment and frustration out on him.

"I like this Marc fellow," he said, before she could speak. He rolled right over whatever she had planned to say, bundling her into her coat and pushing her gently toward the exit. "But I do not like that you would think to encourage the interest of another man, *milka*."

"I wasn't encouraging anything," she groused, standing obediently at his side while the doorman hailed them a cab. "It was just dinner."

"It was a date. And my woman will not date any man but me." The slamming of the taxi door behind them punctuated his words, and chased whatever she had been planning to say right out of her head.

"Your woman?"

In the close confines of the back seat of the taxi, Dmitri reclined beside her, a huge dark presence that threatened to overwhelm her. He leaned close, and Reggie caught the achingly familiar scent of him. Her eyes drifted shut, something she couldn't control, and his lips brushed the high curve of her cheekbone.

"Yes," he murmured in his black velvet voice. "Mine."

Chapter Thirteen

Reggie had attended the opera as a young child—her mother had been a fan—but she'd never before sat in one of the private boxes. She regretted the fact that their seats weren't down in the orchestra where witnesses surrounded them.

She didn't trust Dmitri's pleasant demeanor, not after his demonstration of possessiveness. She kept waiting for the ax to fall.

Looking around while the usher led them to their seats, Reggie reflected on how much safer she would have felt ending this date here with Marc. Even though he had already known about the fantasy, and she would have felt obliged to act it out in this fairly public space, she thought an arrest for public indecency might be less messy than whatever Dmitri had planned.

She let Dmitri take her coat and seat her in one of the two luxurious armchairs that occupied the center of the box. When she looked around her, it almost seemed a shame they were there alone, considering the dimensions of the box could easily have sat four or even six people, oversized chairs not withstanding. And now that she thought about it, viewing the opera with a couple of clear-sighted bystanders might have been a lot safer than being here alone with Dmitri.

The thought echoed in her head while she watched him hand their coats to the usher, who proceeded to move to each side of the box where it bordered their neighbors and release the heavy drapes from their swags. The material formed a visual barrier with the other boxes and made Reggie swallow nervously. The public nature of the box had just been transformed into something else entirely. Something very private.

Centering her attention on the darkened stage, Reggie shifted in her seat and smoothed the silky material of her dress over her thighs. Then she straightened the clasp on her silver and onyx necklace. Then she checked the clasp on her tiny evening bag, gave a tug to her bodice, and smoothed down her hair. When she ran out of fidgets, she stared straight ahead and cursed herself for not wearing opera gloves. They would have provided one more step in her distraction techniques.

The usher left their box, and Dmitri took his seat beside her. She started to tell him he was crowding her, but before she could speak, he slid his arm over the back of her chair and wrapped it around her shoulders. He didn't even pretend the move had been casual. He meant it as a statement of possession, and that's exactly what she took it for. The man was about as subtle as a jackhammer, but she pretended to ignore him and kept her eyes on the stage.

Gratitude washed over her when she saw the house lights dim. Any second the orchestra would finish its warm up, and they would have a legitimate distraction to take their attention.

At least, she would.

The rest of the lights extinguished, and the first notes of the overture flooded through the auditorium. All around them, attention shifted from conversations with companions and strangers to the action revealed on stage when the footlights went up. Everyone watched while the city of Peking came to life before them, and the Mandarin began to sing of the Princess Turandot and the impossible test her suitors must pass in order to win her hand.

In their quiet box high above the stage, Dmitri didn't bother to win Regina's hand. He took it, by right of strength, twining his fingers with hers and resting their clasped hands together on her thigh, halfway between knee and hip.

Oh, Lord.

In her mind, she heard him chuckle.

Titles are archaic, dushka. *And unnecessary. You need not address me so formally. I have told you Misha will do.*

Though she didn't look away from the stage, Reggie felt a rush of relief. He still didn't seem mad at her. Maybe he was going to let this date with Marc thing go after all.

As soon as she relaxed, she couldn't help rolling her eyes. Despite his teasing, the autocratic tenor of his words suited him and rang with an underlying truth. He probably did see himself as some sort of feudal lord, demanding tribute from the peasants while he sat in his castle and counted the spoils of war.

I have always preferred the spoiling to the counting. Mathematics can be so tedious.

Would you be quiet? And get out of my head. I'm trying to watch the opera. Barbarian.

She felt his laughter along with her own sense of satisfaction when he finally deigned to actually look toward the stage.

Of course, milaya. *Because watching the performance was your only intent in coming here tonight.*

He just had to have the last word. She frowned, her attention straying from the touching reunion between the aged Timur and his son, Prince Calaf. Something in his tone made her a little uneasy, but he sat quietly enough beside her, and she soon found herself drawn into the world of the haughty Princess Turandot and her determined suitor, Calaf. The determined part sounded familiar; it was the suitor she was having trouble relating to.

The image of Dmitri petitioning for her hand popped into her brain, and she had to stifle her laugh. Despite Marc calling her a princess, she didn't really think she had much in common with Turandot, but she guaranteed Dmitri was *nothing* like Calaf. He would never follow the dictates of a spoiled princess, never play along with her game. If he wanted her, he would take her, as he had taken Reggie.

The memory of it made her squirm in her seat, and she glanced at him from the corner of her eye. In the dark, she saw the smile curve his gorgeous mouth. She held her breath, waiting for his reaction, but Misha simply raised their joined hands to his lips and brushed a whisper-soft kiss along her knuckles. He turned his attention back to the stage and watched while love battled with anger for the princess's heart.

In Reggie's heart, relief battled with pique to make her decidedly uncomfortable. For some insane reason, she felt disappointed he paid more attention to the stage than to her. What was she thinking? She ought to be relieved the man had decided to behave himself for a change, not brooding he'd been with her for a good hour and hadn't ravished her yet. Clearly, he had driven her over the edge. She could no longer claim to be sane. She needed to get her mind back on the opera and off the hunk at her side.

An hour later, she was still brooding when the houselights came back up for intermission. In fact, she'd been so preoccupied with her thoughts—and memories of their last night together—she'd lost track of the story, and the intermission surprised her. She sat for a moment in the brightened light, blinking while her eyes struggled to adjust.

"Come, *milaya*," Dmitri said when he rose and tugged her to her feet beside him. "Let us stretch our legs for a few moments."

Reggie trailed obediently after him—how did he always manage to make her do that?—as he led her out of the box. They passed other attendees while they walked, women who eyed Dmitri's lean, muscular form with avid appreciation and men who quickly averted their eyes from Reggie's curvaceous figure as soon as they glimpsed Dmitri's threatening scowl.

"Do you have to do that?" Reggie hissed when he dropped his hand to the small of her back to urge her into a reception room ahead of him.

"Do what?"

An opera employee greeted Dmitri by name when they passed. Misha acknowledged the young man with a nod and attempted to sculpt his features into an innocent mask.

"Your dog in the manger routine."

"An inappropriate analogy," he dismissed, accepting two glasses of red wine from the bartender and handing one to her. "While I may have warned a man or two to keep his distance, I assure you that I have no intention of doing the same."

Reggie gazed up into his deep, black eyes, and her stomach flipped. She'd managed to convince herself during the first half of the performance that Dmitri's failure to make her pay for accepting a date with another man meant he no longer felt as interested in her as she was in him. But if she were to judge by the heat of his gaze, she'd have to reassess her conclusion. Rapidly.

Hastily, she raised her glass to her lips and sipped the crisp, dry liquid. Dmitri responded with a smile, but let her enjoy her strategic retreat. He seemed content to watch her take in their surroundings.

As she watched the glittering crowd around them mill about the room, it occurred to Reggie that these weren't your average a-pair-of-tickets-once-in-a-while opera goers. Come to think of it, she felt pretty sure they weren't your average season ticket opera goers.

Oh, my God! Was that a Rockefeller?

Dmitri gazed down at her, clearly amused. *I believe it is. In fact, I'm sure of it, because he is great friends with the Vanderbilt and the Kennedy you see him speaking to.*

She almost choked on her wine. Swallowing quickly, she took another, more searching look around her and felt a little lightheaded. Unless she missed her guess, not one person in the room with her possessed an annual income with less than seven digits. Before the decimal point.

The sound of a woman's rather braying laughter drew her attention, and Reggie looked over to see a well-known television personality conversing with a communications tycoon and two heirs to a real estate fortune. When she examined the quartet in a new light, she realized the tuxedos were definitely not rentals, the gown was a designer original, and the rocks around the TV personality's neck had about as much in common with paste as she had with the people in this room.

Suddenly self-conscious, she glanced down at her hunter-green gown and simple silver jewelry and felt woefully underdressed. She clearly ought to be down in the penny pit with the other peons and not breathing the same rarified air as the debs and celebs up here at the private bar.

"Do not be silly. You have no need for shame. You look magnificent," Dmitri murmured, leaning down so his breath tickled her ear when he spoke.

To the other people in the room, he probably looked like a doting lover, she thought.

"Is that not what I am, *milka*? Your lover?"

Chimes interrupted their dialog and signaled the end of intermission.

Taking her empty glass, he set it alongside his on a small table and returned his hand to the small of her back for the return trip to their box. *Your luck and your timing never cease to astound me,* he drawled into her mind. *I begin to wonder if you have some strange powers of which I am not aware.*

Reggie walked sedately at his side while she mentally used a whip and a chair to subdue the emotions he had wrought inside her. "I think you're just too spoiled and too used to getting your own way," she murmured.

"Ah, but I do always get my way, *milka*, and I see no reason to let that change."

He ushered her into their box and helped her settle into her seat. When he sat beside her, she took another quick look around them followed by a more thorough look at him.

She probably should have noticed it before, but she'd had other things on her mind. The man fairly reeked of privilege. His evening clothes had definitely been custom tailored; there was just no other way he could have gotten the fabric to hug his tall, well-muscled frame that lovingly. His shoes had the buttery soft look of Italian leather, and now that she studied them, she realized his shirt studs and cufflinks shone with the rich, warm glow of solid gold. She'd bet twenty-four carat. Taking a deep breath, she turned back to the stage and crossed her legs primly at the ankles.

Just when the lights began to dim around them, she leaned the tiniest bit closer and, her eyes still fixed on the stage, murmured, "So then, you're pretty much filthy rich, huh?"

"Disgustingly so." He too, kept his attention on the proscenium below.

"Hm. Isn't that special."

Settling back into her seat, she crossed her hands primly in her lap and concentrated on presenting an utterly calm exterior—to contrast with the chaotic thoughts and emotions beneath the surface. Even before this late-breaking news, she'd had a few moments where she wondered exactly what she was doing with Dmitri. After all, the man was drop-dead gorgeous, sexy as sin, dynamite in bed, mysterious as the hero of a gothic romance and one-hundred-percent alpha male. Now she learned he was also richer than Midas. So what the hell had he been doing hanging out at a run of the mill dive like the Mausoleum that night? Why had he fixed his attention on her among all the beautiful women who had been there, available and most likely panting after him? Why had he taken her home and fucked her silly? Why had he cared enough to track her down on a date? What had he been thinking when he kidnapped her away from Marc? Was that his hand under her skirt?

Swallowing a shriek, Reggie jumped about six inches off her chair when Dmitri's warm, bare hand snaked around her waist, tugged her close and proceeded to slip under her skirt and glide purposefully up her inner thigh.

"Just what do you think you're doing?" she demanded in a hissing whisper.

"Apparently something you need to become a bit more familiar with, if you can't recognize when I am making love to you, *dushka*." He laughed against her ear, his other hand covering both of hers and holding them still. "You see, this," his hands skimmed over her soft flesh, discovered her lack of panties and petted her in approval, "is me making love to you. And this," his hand shifted, and he penetrated her with one long finger, his way made slick and easy by her moisture, "is you enjoying it."

Overwhelmed by the sound of his voice like a dark caress against her ear and his finger slowly stroking in and out of her tight cunt, Reggie struggled to bite back a moan with only partial success. Frantic, she looked around, but the curtains at the sides of the box were still drawn, and the boxes at the opposite side of the auditorium were too far away to see into in the dim light. No one could possibly see what they were doing, what Dmitri was doing to her, but if he kept it up, they might very well be able to hear.

She tried to tug her hands free, but his grip only tightened. When she tried to squirm her hips away, he only added a second finger and pressed his thumb against her clit.

"Stop!" She breathed the plea, afraid to speak any louder, almost afraid to speak at all. She could feel the moans welling up in her throat and bit the inside of her cheek to keep from letting them out.

"But you do not want me to stop, *dushka*." His breath was hot against her ear, his teeth hard and gentle when he bit down on her lobe and made her cunt spasm around his fingers. "You want me to continue. You want me to take you higher. You want me to fulfill your fantasies."

Reggie froze, every muscle in her body going taut and still. What did he know about her fantasies? He'd said something similar to her during their night together, hadn't he? As if he knew what she dreamed about, her secrets, her desires.

"Don't I?" His hand twisted, fingers curling to stroke the sensitive inner walls of her pussy, thumb rubbing a torturous circle against her throbbing clit. "Don't I give you what you want, Regina?"

He forced a third finger inside her, stretching her wide and leaving her wildly aroused. A whimper almost choked her, and she bit her lip. She knew his eyes watched her face while he pleasured her, but she couldn't focus on him. She couldn't focus on anything but his touch.

She felt when her teeth first pierced her own skin. The intensity of her reaction to him frightened her, but she couldn't pull away, not when her cunt ached to get closer. The pain of her torn lip couldn't distract her, nor could the drop of crimson blood that welled up from the broken skin. Through her daze, she heard Misha growl deep in his chest. His head swooped down, and his mouth settled over hers.

His tongue darted out to lick the blood away, soothing the tiny wound with his caress. He took her mouth, filling her, overwhelming her with his taste and his touch and his scent. She went under like a poor swimmer in deep water, tugged down by the undertow of his passion. With his tongue in her mouth and his fingers in her cunt, he encompassed her, as if she were an ornament he wore or a puppet that moved only at the command of his touch.

Misha, she thought, because in the chaotic swirl of emotion and sensation, his name remained the only thread that linked her to reality. He had become the universe in which she existed, the air in her lungs and blood in her veins. *Misha, please.*

And he pleased her. Sucking her lip with almost tender tugs, he shifted his hand again, his thumb sliding up until the edge of his nail pressed against the top of her slit and the ball of his thumb applied delicate, stuttering pressure against her clit. His fingers inside her thrust and massaged and pushed her right over the edge. She melted around him, pussy weeping, muscles clenching, breath halted in a great, shuddering, silent orgasm that threatened to overwhelm her even when she wished for it to never end.

But eventually, the spasms faded. Her muscles eased, and her breath started again in shallow pants. His fingers eased out of her and feathered through her curls, petting her like a kitten that needed soothing. Frankly, it wasn't doing much to slow her heart rate, and neither were the teasing kisses he'd taken to planting along her jaw line.

She drew in a shuddering breath and closed her eyes, no longer even pretending to watch the performers. Her world had just been turned upside down, and somehow the romantic tribulations of a spoiled brat in a fictionalized, medieval China couldn't compare with the real life adventures of her experiences with Dmitri. Good lord, just imagine an opera about them!

"I believe it would be illegal to perform in most countries," he murmured, nuzzling the hollow beneath her ear and smiling. "Such things are still generally considered ill-suited for public consumption." She blushed hot enough to burn, and he drew back to grin down at her, licking her juices from his fingers. "Though the audience would surely fall in love with whatever actress portrayed you, *dushka*, especially if she blushed as prettily as you do when she came."

Embarrassed to her pink-polished toes, Reggie decided Misha had fallen a bit too easily into the roll of charming, self-controlled rogue. He definitely needed to get a little of his own back.

She took a moment to check up on the action on stage and threw a glance at her watch, thankful there was enough light to see. It looked like they had about forty-minutes left until the end of the performance, which should be just enough time for a little judicious revenge. Her lips curved in anticipation.

For the next several moments she pretended to be absorbed by the story on stage. In reality, she was waiting for Dmitri to relax and shift his own attention off of her even briefly. It took a few minutes, but finally he seemed to content himself with once again holding her hand in his, and he watched while lack of sleep began to wear on the fictional people of Peking.

She started by leaning closer to him, snuggling against his side and laying her cheek on the warm silk of his lapel. She shifted their clasped hands from her thigh to his and stilled and waited. His arm slipped around her shoulder to cradle her to him, and she thought she felt his lips brush over her hair, but he continued to watch the stage.

After a few more minutes, she cast a furtive glance around to be sure no one could see into their little boxed-in cocoon and took a deep breath. Time to make her move.

With a feather light touch, Reggie slipped one of her hands free and sent it gliding up Dmitri's inner thigh, mirroring the move he'd made over her bare skin earlier. Unfortunately, due to the nature of men's fashions, cloth muffled her touch, but she could still feel his muscles bunch and tighten beneath her hand. When she reached the vee of his legs, she skirted her fingers around the very interesting bulge behind his fly and headed straight up to the hook at the top. Slipping it free of its catch, she grasped the zipper between her fingers and waited. She felt his anticipation as keenly as his heartbeat that pulsed against the back of her hand. When the secondary soprano hit an extended high note, Reggie tugged and lowered the zipper. Her hand slid under the straining cloth and found him, warm and hard and heavy beneath. Her murmur expressed her approval and her fingers gladly curled around his cock, feeling the flesh twitch and throb against her palm.

Leisurely, she began to stroke him, scraping her fingernails delicately against the skin at the base of the shaft and squeezing lightly when she moved toward the tip. She tortured him with a few of the teasing strokes, or at least, she meant them to be teasing, but a quick glance at his face revealed no particular strain. He looked way too calm for her tastes. Eyes narrowing, she continued to watch him while she tightened her grip, pumping his cock in her small fist and using her index finger to rub circles around the sensitive head. His cock twitched, but his face remained impassive. This meant war.

In a flash of movement she slid off her seat and onto her knees before him to suck the head of his cock between her lips. That at least made him draw in a deep breath, but when he let it out, he wore the same polite expression he'd used during the entire opera. Well, Reggie would show him what being a virtuoso was all about.

Drawing her long hair to one side and draping the length over her shoulder, she freed her other hand from his grip and spread open his evening trousers. She wrapped one hand around the base of his cock and used the other to lift his balls from their confinement, cuddling them tenderly in her palm. Watching him from beneath her eyelashes, she leaned forward and delicately nibbled the skin of his glans.

Dmitri shuddered.

Reggie smiled. The man just might not be made of stone after all, she mused, though you'd never know it from his cock. He felt hard as granite, but infinitely warmer. His pulse throbbed against her lips, and she parted them to take the first few inches into her mouth, closing around him like a moist heaven. One hand continued to cradle and massage his balls, and the other wrapped around the base of his shaft, stroking what she couldn't fit in her mouth.

Dmitri watched the stage.

Acknowledging the challenge, Reggie applied herself to her task, and a very pleasant one, she found it. His cock filled her mouth, the thickness stretching her jaw just enough to make her acutely aware of what she was doing. He pressed against her tongue, filling her with his salty, earthy, intensely masculine flavor. He smelled the same, fresh and clean and earthy, the essence of a man, like forests after spring rain showers. Humming her approval, she suckled his cock like a tasty treat, and he rewarded her with a hiss of indrawn breath.

Yes, milka. Sosi mne. *Suck me.*

Reggie did, her head bobbing while she drew his cock deep into her mouth and released him, over and over, swirling her tongue around the head with each pass. Her eyes had drifted shut, but she felt his hands sink into her hair and cup the back of her head, holding her to him. The possessive gesture excited her.

Bystraye. *Faster.*

She worked faster, tightening her hand at the base of his shaft, massaging his balls with a firmer motion. He pressed against her tongue, his cock hardening even more, if that were possible. His hands clenched in her hair and even the small pain of it aroused her. She whimpered, the sound muffled around his cock, then hummed in the back of her throat so the vibrations traveled through her tongue and palate to provide another layer to the sensation that already threatened to send him over the edge.

Ah! Bozhe moy, ya umirayu! *My God, I'm dying!*

Even in his thoughts, Reggie sensed his urgency. A moment later, his cock heated and throbbed and suddenly he filled her mouth with sperm, the thick, milky liquid overwhelming her. She tried to pull back, but his hands remained fisted in her hair. She struggled, and he untangled one, sliding it around to cup her face.

Zagloti, dushka. *Swallow for me, baby. There's a good girl.*

Reggie obeyed. His hand on her skin and the tenderness in his tone soothed her, made the alien experience seem safer and less threatening. Though she'd never swallowed the results of any of her previous blowjobs, she swallowed this one, and felt somehow that the act brought her closer to her lover.

When she finished, he adjusted his clothing and pulled her back up to her seat to kiss her, his dark eyes glinting in reflected stage lights. "Thank you, *milaya*."

Suddenly shy—which was ridiculous considering what she'd just been doing—Reggie smiled at him and snuggled against his side. He wrapped his strong arms around her and held her close, resting his chin on top of her head while Turandot wept with joy at Calaf's kiss.

Reggie watched the scene on stage and smiled against Dmitri's lapel. Turandot might think her prince was hot stuff, but she clearly didn't know what she was missing.

Chapter Fourteen

Nerves attacked Reggie when she watched Dmitri unlock the door to his gorgeous, old brownstone townhouse. She'd spent the last few minutes at the opera and the entire cab ride here in a dazed sort of contentment, feeling so warm and foggy she'd never noticed when the taxi took them in the opposite direction from her apartment. It dropped them off in a hideously expensive, historic neighborhood on the Upper East Side in front of the building Misha now ushered her into.

The golden glow of the entry lights gleamed on the warm, hardwood floors and period wainscoted walls. Above the paneling, the walls were papered in the sort of embossed wall covering that had more in common with expensive fabric than generic wallpaper. She tore her eyes away from the artwork on the wall (which *really* looked like an original Degas charcoal sketch), and let Dmitri take her coat. He draped it along with his over a settee and took her arm.

"Welcome to my home, *dushka*," he said formally. He stared down at her and tucked a stray curl behind her ear. "You honor me with your presence."

Reggie gulped and fidgeted, suddenly feeling unsure and out of place. "I think the Queen of England would have a hard time honoring this place. I think I'm just lucky the elegance police have given me a get out of jail free card."

His lips quirked. "You have a very expansive sort of leeway in my home, *dushka*. You may do anything you wish here. Except, perhaps, to leave."

He meant she couldn't leave tonight.

Didn't he?

"I would give you a tour," he continued, guiding her inexorably toward the stairs, "but I am afraid it is not possible at the moment."

"Your maid had the day off?"

"I cannot wait another five minutes to be inside you again."

Oh. Right. Well, then.

She found herself up the stairs and down the hall before she could digest his comment, let alone decide what to do about it. He pushed open a heavy, paneled door, and she got a brief glimpse of a massive expanse of mattress edged with carved posts and dark, silken sheets before she found herself swept up into his arms and carried across the floor. She clung to his broad shoulders, her head whirling, until he laid her on her back atop the cool sheets and pressed her arms down beside her head. He loomed over her, a great, heated shadow that blocked her view of anything else, not that anything else mattered.

"Did you miss me, *milaya*?" he demanded, his voice a stir of gravel and sin. "While we were apart, did your body ache for me?"

His hand slid down to palm her breast for an instant before it continued over her stomach to cup her through the fabric of her dress. "Did you dream of me?"

His touch drove the breath from her lungs. She arched her body, pressing herself against his hand.

God, if he only knew what she had dreamed.

"Tell me."

She tried, she really did, but the only sound she could make was a whimpering sort of gasp when he touched her. Her eyes drifted shut, and her lids became a screen on which the film of her fantasies ran in all their Technicolor glory.

She heard Dmitri laugh, a low, rumbling sound. "Ah, *milaya*, you are a wonder to me. You have such passion behind your conventional little exterior." His hand moved to the zipper at the back of her dress. "It pleases me."

The material gave way beneath his hands, and he tugged the dress away from her and tossed it aside, leaving her sprawled out before him in lewd abandon. She'd gone naked beneath the dress, since the bodice had a built in bra, and he'd ordered her to forgo panties, so now all she wore was her pale skin, her white flesh a stark contrast to the darkness of the man looming over her. She opened her eyes and found him staring, his glance like a pair of hands running over her, raising gooseflesh on her skin.

"Lovely," he murmured. He released her hands and sat back, resting against the carved headboard with indolent grace. "But I think I am intrigued by this dream you have had of me, *dushka*. I would like to make it come true for you. And for me."

His eyes glinted with an intensity his lazy drawl had managed to conceal. Reggie twisted into a sitting position and faced him. He raised his eyebrow and remained still. A thrill of excitement ran through her. He expected to lay back and be pleasured, like some pasha with his slave girl, and Reggie's normally independent nature remained cheerfully silent, offering not a single protest. It shocked her to realize these fantasies of hers—these submissive feelings she'd always felt were so antithetical to her real personality and beliefs—maybe they weren't so foreign to her nature after all. They certainly felt completely natural in that moment.

Taking a deep breath, she scooted forward across the mattress until she knelt before him, perched hesitantly between his thighs. She reached up to his collar and tugged loose the knot in his tie. Silk whispered against silk when she drew the fabric free and tossed it on the floor beside the bed. Dmitri merely smiled.

Her fingers fumbled a little on his shirt studs, but eventually she got the tiny gold clasps unfastened. When she started to slide off the bed so she could set the studs down on the bedside table, Dmitri fastened his hands around her waist and stopped her.

You are not permitted to get up just now.

Reggie read his challenge in his eyes. Once he knew she understood, he dropped his hands. Nibbling her lower lip, Reggie hesitated for a second. She braced one hand against the mattress and leaned across him. If she stretched as far as she could without tumbling over, she could just reach to drop the studs on the edge of the table. Stretching in that direction, though, meant she had to drape herself across Dmitri's torso, bringing her breasts within an inch or two of his face.

He noticed. His lips latched onto her nipple and tugged in a sweet suckling motion. Reggie moaned, a shiver of pleasure shaking her. Blindly, she groped for the nightstand and dropped the studs onto the corner. She vaguely heard them make contact with the wooden surface and fall, scattering across the floor with tiny pinging noises. She couldn't have cared less. She wrapped her arms around Dmitri's head, pressing him closer to her. As soon as she did so, he pulled back.

"How clumsy of you, Regina," he murmured, pushing her back to a kneeling position in front of him. "I expect you to take better care of my things. I trust you will not be so cavalier with my cufflinks." He extended his arm to her, wrist turned to expose the decorative clasp.

Reggie hurried to unfasten it, repeating the operation with the other cuff. She leaned forward toward the nightstand, but this time she twisted her body so she presented Dmitri with her shoulder blade, rather than her breasts. If he went for her nipples again, she'd be totally useless.

She heard him chuckle, and his hand slid swiftly between her legs, penetrating her with two long fingers. She froze in place, dropping her head on a groan. "Are you trying to kill me?"

"Only in the French sense of the word, *dushka. Seulement la petite morte.*"

"Oh. Only a little death," she translated in her high school French, panting while she set the cufflinks carefully on the table. "I feel so much better now."

Dmitri laughed, his lips brushing against her nipple as he brought his thumb into play, using it to draw tight little circles around her already aching clit. *No, no,* milaya. La petite morte *is…well, allow me to demonstrate.*

His free hand slid to her side, cupping one breast and shifting her to face him fully. He raked his thumbnail over the erect nipple even while his teeth nibbled delicately at the bud in his mouth. Reggie shuddered and tried to pull away, but succeeded only in pressing herself harder on the hand between her legs. His fingers sank deeper, and he curled the tips to caress the inner walls of her pussy. She felt trapped and overwhelmed and dizzy with the sensations pounding at her. She grabbed desperately at his shoulders, needing an anchor to hold her steady. The pressure inside her built with ridiculous speed, winding tighter and faster with each stroke of his fingers, each glide of his tongue. She became an extension of his touch, existing only for the fingers in her cunt and the mouth on her breast.

"Misha," she whimpered, feeling him guide her inexorably to the edge of an enormous cliff. What would happen when he drove her over, she couldn't imagine. "Please. I-I need…"

I know, milaya. *I know.* His thumb pressed harder on her clit, and his fingers closed sharply around her nipple. *Come for me,* dushka. *Now.*

She obeyed, her body drawing tight while the tension inside her peaked and broke, flooding her with pleasure and flooding his hand with the evidence. She slid boneless against him, leaning her cheek against the front of his shirt while her hands still clutched at his shoulders.

She struggled to catch her breath, shuddering delicately with the aftershocks that still rippled through her. Dmitri comforted her, petting her back with soothing motions and brushing soft kisses against her hair. He gave her a few minutes to compose herself, but his hands soon moved to her hips and sat her back on her heels again.

"I do not believe you had yet finished your task, Regina," he said, glancing down at his shirt, which hung open but still covered his arms and broad shoulders. "I would not want to think you neglect your chores."

Because undressing him is such a chore, she thought, biting her cheek to keep from rolling her eyes. She waited for one of his smart comments, but Dmitri remained silent. He was waiting.

Sliding her hands beneath the two, open shirt halves, Reggie took her time, savoring the warm weight of his muscular chest beneath her hands. She savored the feel of him, smooth and hard near his shoulders, rougher and somehow less civilized in the center of his chest where a blanket of masculine fur arrowed down toward his waistband. She leaned forward to strip the cloth from his shoulders and gave in to the temptation to rub her cheek against the sensual, contrasting textures. She felt the rippling of his muscles beneath her touch, but he kept his hands at his sides and let her continue.

She pushed the shirt down his arms and tugged it from under him, tossing it away near his tie. She sat back to survey what she'd uncovered.

Great googly-moogly. Lord, but the man was gorgeous. He had the musculature of a Greek statue that had decided to take up bodybuilding. She could see the definition of his muscles when they flexed and shifted, and appreciated they stopped short of exaggeration. His shoulders looked impossibly broad while he lounged there in graceful splendor. His chest was wide and strong, his waist lean and stomach firm. And suddenly she couldn't wait to see the rest of him again.

The fingers she lifted to his waistband trembled before she managed to force them into steadiness. Just to be sure they were prepared to obey her, she caressed them down his sides, her thumbs brushing over his nipples before gliding south to his tuxedo pants. She undid the top catch and gripped the zipper tab between her thumb and forefinger and slowly began inching the fastening open. Her eyes were glued to her task, her head bowed, the tension of a child on Christmas morning surrounding her. She felt his eyes on her while she pulled the zipper down the last few millimeters and spread open his fly.

He wore nothing beneath but his skin, a fact she'd appreciated at the opera and reveled in now. She tugged at the fabric, and he cooperated by lifting his hips so she could pull it down. She eased back toward the foot of the bed, stopped just past his feet and quickly stripped them as well. Grabbing hold of his slacks, she tugged them down and off of him, casting them aside behind her. She lowered her head, set her tongue against the hollow of his ankle and slowly dragged it upward along the inside of his leg.

She loved the taste of him, warm and salty and solid. He tasted like man and earth and desire, and she paused occasionally on her journey to enjoy the flavor. He let her have her way and lay still beneath her lazy exploration, but she heard his breath catch when she reached his knee and stroked her tongue along the crease behind it. When she reached his thighs, he gave in and buried his hands in her hair, fingers massaging her scalp while her tongue darted out to stroke the smooth skin she found there. Here his taste was stronger, darker, even more enticing. She let her tongue glide up and up until it flicked over his balls in a warm hello.

Her eyes drifted shut in pleasure, and she rubbed her cheek against his erection like a cat, enjoying the knowledge she'd caused him to harden, that she had brought him pleasure and made him want. She parted her lips to take him inside, but he had other plans. Grasping her arms, he dragged her up, bare skin sliding over bare skin, until her face came level with his.

His black eyes gleamed in the candlelight—candles that hadn't been lit a moment ago—and his lips curved in a wicked smile. "Not this time, *dushka*," he whispered, brushing his lips against hers, returning a heartbeat later for a deeper kiss. He nibbled her lips apart, stroked her tongue with his, conquered her mouth and claimed her for his own. When he drew back, her breathing had turned into excited panting. "I have seen your desire for me, seen how you dreamed of me. That is what I want from you now. Will you indulge me?"

Reggie didn't answer, but she figured since he could read her mind somehow, he could probably see the excitement there. Did he think she'd argue with the man who was well on his way to fulfilling every single one of her hottest sexual fantasies? She wasn't *totally* out of her mind.

Leaning down she brushed her lips against his, against his throat, his nipples and the tip of his cock. She sat up and turned her back to him, kneeling between his spread legs and bracing her hands against his hard thighs. She perched on her heels, her back straight and graceful before him, and turned to send him an enticing look over her shoulder.

Dmitri rumbled out a sound of appreciation. He moved closer and slid his hands over the smooth skin of her back, briefly cupping her ass before he wrapped his arms around her and pressed against her.

"You are so lovely, *milka*," he murmured, and his breath tickled her ear even while his hands slid up to cuddle her full breasts in his palms. "Soft and lush and sweet." His tongue flicked her earlobe, followed by gentle nibbles, and one of his hands slid down the center of her body, over the soft curve of her stomach and down between her thighs. "Warm and wet and giving."

His fingers slipped easily over her damp flesh, tracing each curve and fold, probing at her entrance as if testing her readiness. God, how could he doubt she was ready for him?

"It pleases me that you take pleasure in my pleasure," he whispered, sinking two fingers deep inside her. "You were made for me. Can you not tell?"

He trailed kisses from the hollow behind her ear, along her throat to the curve of her shoulder. Reggie's head fell back, resting on his shoulder while he sent waves and waves of pleasure coursing through her.

"Can you not tell you were born for me, Regina? Born to please me and to be pleasured by me?"

Reggie groaned, her mind blank of everything but Misha and pleasure and need. Her fingers tightened on his thighs, dug into his flesh, her whole body tensed with wanting. "Misha. Please."

"Can you tell, Regina?"

His black magic voice only added to the chaos inside her, only layered another level of sensation on her already-overloaded nervous system. Her body arched, pressing into his hands. "God! Misha, I want…"

His hand at her breast abandoned its massage and slid up her shoulder to the nape of her neck. His fingers caressed her briefly before they firmed on her skin and pressed, urging her forward. She followed his silent command, easing forward to brace her weight on her hands and lift her hips, until she knelt on all fours before him and trembled.

He bracketed her hips with both hands and leaned over her, covering her with his heat and his presence. His lips brushed the nape of her neck, making her shudder. She could feel his lips curve into a smile.

"What do you want, *dushka*?" He teased her, knowing the answer, but forcing her to say it.

Reggie's head bowed, her long hair falling forward to curtain her from everything else. She didn't know if she could talk, didn't know if she still controlled her body, since it seemed so intent on doing Misha's bidding. She tested her tongue, tried to speak. Nothing emerged but a whimper, and she pressed back against him instead, her ass cushioning the pulsing length of his cock.

His hands pressed her forward, separating their flesh. She groaned at the loss of the contact.

"What is it you want?"

Reggie moaned and tried to sit up, to turn toward him, but his hand just cupped the back of her neck again and pressed her back down. This time he held her there while he repeated the question. "What do you want, Regina?"

Frustration and the pain of wanting him gave her the power to speak, barely. Her words tore from her on a moan. "You! God, Misha, I want *you*!"

He hummed his approval, and his hand lifted from her neck. It trailed down the length of her spine, slid between them. His cock nudged at the opening of her cunt, demanding entrance. She wanted him to thrust, needed him to fuck her, needed to feel him inside her. But he wasn't done torturing her.

"I can feel what you want, Regina," he crooned, his hands reaching to cup her breasts where they hung beneath her. He pressed against her back, her cunt, her breasts. She felt surrounded by him, overwhelmed and helpless. And, Lord, but it felt good. His breath caressed her cheek, and he nuzzled her hair out of his way so he could touch his skin to hers.

"But what are you willing to give me in return?"

Moaning and shaking and needing him more than her next breath, Reggie turned her head enough to touch her mouth to his. Parting her lips against his, she breathed her answer into his mouth, as if she could gift her soul to him.

"Anything," she whispered urgently, willing him to know how much she meant it. " I would give you anything."

"Yes."

He took her mouth, claimed it, marked it as his. His tongue swept over hers like a conquering warrior, even though her surrender came swift and willing. When he finally drew back, she could see his intensity and his lust in the harsh cast of his features. His savage look caused her no fear, but made her tremble with the thrill of anticipation.

"You will give me everything, *dushka*," he growled, hands grabbing her hips to hold her still. "And I will take all you have. For you are *mine*."

As he spoke, he thrust, claiming her physically even as he claimed her verbally. Reggie gasped at the intrusion, her body shocked at the feel of him after a weeklong absence. Her muscles clenched to ward him off, but it was much too late. He was already buried to the hilt, his thick cock stretching her, pleasure and discomfort blending into an indistinguishable maelstrom of sensation.

He released her hips long enough to grab her wrists and guide her hands to the rail at the foot of the bed. She had to stretch to reach it, moving forward on her knees until she leaned past them, shifting her center of gravity to her torso and throwing herself off balance. Misha followed her motion, embedded in her clutching pussy, and wrapped her hands around the cool wood, squeezing a warning that she leave them there. The position was awkward. Her weight had shifted forward and now was supported mainly by her grip on the railing and Dmitri's grip on her hips. If she moved, she would collapse. All she could do was kneel there, still and submissive, and let him take her.

He did.

He leaned forward to place a tender kiss on her spine just at the small of her back. He reared back, withdrawing until only the head of his cock remained inside her; then he braced her hips before him, and plunged.

Reggie screamed. She barely heard herself, too caught up in the feel of him pounding inside of her. Her head jerked back even as the force of his thrust pushed her forward. She braced her arms, locking herself in place, not wanting to lose even a pound of the force. She tried to spread her legs further to give herself a better sense of balance, but his calves were braced on the outside of hers to keep her exactly as he had positioned her. All she could do was whimper and accept him.

He drew back slowly, making her pant. She could feel each inch of him while it pulled out of her, feel her cunt collapsing back on itself, relieved of the huge, invading cock. It felt like a massage on her most sensitive tissues. She thought wildly that nothing could feel better, but he surged forward again, filled her again, and she knew how wrong she had been.

Misha settled into a rhythm, fast and hard and desperately deep. Each thrust brought him inside her to the hilt. She could feel his balls swing against her, feel his cock butting against her cervix. She'd never been fucked this deep, this hard. She loved it, wanted more, and even while she thought it, he gave it to her.

"Misha!"

She screamed his name. Her body shook with his thrusts. The tension was unbearable. She needed him to stop. She needed him to never stop. She needed to get away. She needed to get closer. Her hands clenched so hard on the bedrail that her knuckles ached. Her elbows had locked, stretched out before her, and she used her braced position to thrust herself back onto his cock, desperate to take everything he had.

He obliged her with a grunt, and somehow he grew impossibly larger inside her, stretching her abused pussy even further. She shuddered, and her head fell. Her hands remained braced on the railing, but her upper body sank down until she rested her cheek and her shoulder on the mattress, her hips still angled up to take Misha's fierce, pounding sex.

She gulped in oxygen, desperate and out of breath. If he didn't stop, he would kill her. If he ever stopped, she'd die.

Misha leaned forward, curling his body around hers, his hips still hammering hard and rhythmically into her. She felt the slight roughness of his cheek against the sensitive skin of her neck, heard the irregular sound of his breathing, felt the heat of him like a firebrand against her.

She heard his voice, deep and harsh and frighteningly intense.

"What would you give me, *dushka*?" he growled low and bestial.

Reggie tried to moan, but she didn't even have the breath for that. She couldn't speak, couldn't think, could barely hold herself up for his possession.

Anything, she thought desperately. *I would give you anything!*

Anything?

Everything.

She heard a rumbling growl of pleasure, felt him shift, fill her more deeply, surround her more completely. She felt a sharp pain at her throat, and she shattered.

The pleasure inside her exploded and she came, spasming around his thrusting cock, milking him of his seed, sharing her ecstasy, as she had shared her body. The orgasm lasted forever, her pussy clenching in time to the rhythmic draw on her pulse. She felt him tense, heard another muffled growl when he spurted inside her, still feeding on her pleasure as he fed on her blood.

Chapter Fifteen

She woke and was astounded. Her memory possessed the crystalline clarity of a movie reel. She knew exactly what had happened to her, and quite frankly, the last thing she'd expected had been to wake up again.

I fucked a vampire.

"Actually, I believe if you wished to be technical, the vampire fucked you."

Reggie shot up in bed, one hand clutching the silken sheet to her chest while the other slapped down over the bruise on her neck. "I'm not dead."

"Not at all." Dmitri pushed away from the doorframe where he'd been lounging and watching her sleep. He'd pulled on a pair of worn black jeans, but nothing else.

Reggie stared helplessly at his chest and cursed herself for the lust that surged through her. Not only had the man sucked her blood like a Slurpee, but he'd fucked her so hard, she still felt tender. She had no business getting all wet at the thought of him doing it again.

"You're perfectly healthy," he assured her, perching on the edge of the bed and wrapping a hand around her ankle when she would have moved away. "Not to mention tasty."

"You ought to know," she grumbled, inspecting the hand she'd pressed to her neck for signs of residual bleeding.

"Dry as a bone," he assured her, looking amused. "The wounds close up almost immediately. I did leave you with a little hickey, though. I could have fed without marking you, but I found the idea of you bearing my 'love bite' too amusing to resist."

"Har-har." Reggie stared at him and waited for the panic to flood her. It didn't happen. All she felt when she looked at him was horny. Well, horny and wary. He *was* a bloodsucking fiend, after all, but he didn't seem to have killed her, and what's done was done. Which meant it was probably a good time to ask a few questions.

"Did you turn me into one of you?" she demanded, crossing her arms over her chest and scooting back to lean against the headboard. Might as well get comfortable before she turned into a bat or something.

"Of course not. More is required to make a vampire than a simple bite. If that were all it took, the world would be overrun—by us 'bloodsucking fiends.'"

He appeared more amused than insulted, but Reggie was distracted by another revelation. "That's why you can read my mind! You've got some vampiric power of mind control, or something."

Dmitri chuckled. "Or something. I cannot control your mind, *milka*. I can influence your decisions, but only in the direction your subconscious already wishes to go. If I could truly control you, you never would have attempted to date that Marc person. But I can read your thoughts, and I can speak to you in your mind."

"Can you read everyone's mind? Can I?" Now that could be a useful little skill.

"You can read only me, unless you have other talents you have been hiding from me," he teased. "Were you to become like me, your talents would strengthen with time. I can read your mind with true clarity. Some others I can read fairly easily, some barely at all. I do get impressions from most humans, though. I am an infallible judge of character."

"Too bad I'm not."

He reached out and tucked a lock of hair behind her ear. "I am really not an evil monster, *dushka*. I am just a man who has lived an unusually long life."

"Yeah, and who lives off drinking other people's blood. That hardly sounds like Prince Charming." She scowled at him.

"The Prince is a fairy tale. I am real, and I do drink blood to survive. I am not ashamed of it. I do not kill those I drink from, and I do them no lasting harm. I have lived too many years not to be at peace with what I am, Regina."

Reggie really wanted to ask how long he *had* lived, but his talk of "lasting harm" had brought a more pressing issue to her mind. "So you're sure I'm not a vampire now?"

He grinned. "Positive. In order to become a vampire, you would need to drink from me as I have drunk from you. Unless that happens, you remain my very human, very stubborn, very adorable Regina."

"Flattery is not going to sweep this all under the rug, bucko." She humphed to cover up the warm fuzzies his words gave her. "You are a vampire. That's big news in my world. I don't generally date the living dead."

"What sort of dead do you usually date?" He ducked her punch and laughed. "I'm really not all that different than any other man. I have the needs any man has."

And then some, she thought, shifting her weight and feeling the evidence of the "some" she'd experienced a few hours ago. "Other men don't drink blood," she insisted.

"No, but among human men there are those who are greater monsters than I am. I would never hurt you, *milaya*. You are precious to me."

That brought the fuzzies back, but she ignored them. One thing at a time. She needed more information. "You *could* hurt me, though. You're really strong, and fast as hell. I've seen you move."

Dmitri shrugged. "I am a man. I could have hurt you when I was human. But yes, being a vampire does give me additional strength and speed. Still, these are things I would never use to harm you."

"What else can you do?"

"Am I a trick pony?"

She scowled. "You know what I mean. Like, are you going to turn into a bat or something?"

He rolled his eyes. "Why would I want to transform myself into a disease-carrying, winged rodent?"

"How should I know? I can't understand why you would want to drink blood."

His eyes fastened on the curve of bare skin where her neck met her shoulder, and all of a sudden his expression turned from lazy amusement to heated interest. "Ah, but your blood is intoxicating, *milaya*. Shall I describe for you its sweetness? Its warmth? The way it goes to my head like aged whiskey?" He met her gaze, and his eyes filled with wicked intent. "Shall I describe the cries you give when I drink from you?"

She remembered coming apart in his arms with his fangs and his cock all buried inside her, and she blushed. "Don't change the subject. I'm trying to get some answers. I want to know exactly what I've gotten myself into here."

Dmitri sighed and stretched out on his back beside her. He bore a look of long-suffering as he closed his eyes and began to recite facts. "You have watched too many movies and read some lurid novels," he said. "Vampires are not the monsters humans like to portray us as. We are different by our very natures, but we are no better and no worse as vampires than we were as men. We are stronger and faster, this is true. Our senses are also keener, and our lifetimes can be prolonged indefinitely. In order to survive, we must drink blood. But we are not harmed by crosses or garlic or holy water or any of that nonsense. We can be killed if you destroy our hearts, for that is the organ that supplies our bodies with the blood we consume. And, of course, if you behead us we will also die. I know of few things that could live without their heads."

"Few?" Reggie squeaked, so floundering for a grip on reality she could only focus on one statement at a time, and that had been the last one. "You mean there are things that can?"

"I always assumed politicians could do so. They so seldom seem to use them."

Her jaw dropped open for a second, until she noticed he had cracked one eye open so he could watch her reaction to his teasing. She closed her mouth with a snap and glared at him. Somehow the things he told her actually reassured her. She couldn't understand why, but her reality had just shifted and found a new foundation. Her belief system had made room for an unexpected addition, and now things looked to be getting back to normal.

If you could call having a flaming affair with a vampire "normal."

Reggie scooted down a bit and turned on her side to face him, propping her head in one hand, the other maintaining a firm grip on the sheet. "Wooden stake and sunlight?" she asked, her tone now more curious than frightened.

"If you drove a wood stake through the heart of any living thing, I imagine it would not live much longer," he said, turning to mirror her position. He didn't touch her, but somehow she felt the intimacy of his company. "And sunlight is painful, but not usually life threatening. We cannot absorb the melanin in the blood we drink," he explained. "And we do not produce our own. Therefore, we burn easily. But I have yet to burst into flame."

She humphed. The man had a way with sarcasm. "So, basically you're telling me you're a totally average guy with superhuman strength, the ability to read my mind and a very selective diet."

He grinned at her. "Precisely."

"And you'll never grow old or die."

"It is unlikely to happen for a very long time."

Her death grip on the covers loosened. "Don't you get bored? I mean, after a century or two, I'd think you'd have seen it all."

"I have many varied interests that keep my attention," he informed her, still grinning. "Human culture is a fascinating thing. It evolves constantly and with dizzying speed. And if you wish to know my age, you have only to ask me."

Apparently, her fishing hadn't been as subtle as she'd thought. "Fine. How old are you?"

"I was born in Kiev, as I told your date this evening." His eyes met hers, and that damned eyebrow quirked again. "In the year 1243."

Reggie shrieked and leapt from the bed, dragging the sheet with her. Or at least, that's what she tried to do, but since Dmitri still lay on top of it, the sheet refused to budge. All she was able to take with her was the corner, which barely managed to cover the vitals—a fact Misha noted with apparent approval.

"You're seven-hundred and sixty years old?!?!?"

Misha clearly decided to ignore the fact that she sounded like a fishwife. He merely raised that eyebrow and reached down to give a light tug at the sheet. "Seven hundred and fifty-nine," he corrected calmly. "The anniversary of my birth is not until October."

"Oh, well, pardon me. That makes everything perfectly all right. Those few months are incredibly important to me. I'd hate it if I broke my rule of not dating older men by that wide a margin."

"Sarcasm does not become you, *milka*. Besides, what does my age matter? Do I look seven-hundred-fifty-nine?"

"Of course not. But that…that's not just old—not just dead—it's compost!"

He tugged harder at the sheet, beginning to look impatient. "And I am very much alive and very much desirous of touching you again. Come back to bed."

"I'm not ready to," she scowled, digging her heels into the soft oriental carpet under her feet. "I've still got questions."

"You can ask them later. Right now, I have more important things to do."

He gave one hard tug on the sheet, so fast Reggie had no time to let go. She went tumbling forward and landed right in his arms. He had her on the bed and underneath him again so fast she felt dizzy.

"Misha, cut it out!" He tossed the sheet away, pinned her arms over her head with one hand, and set about torturing her with teasing licks and nibbles that trailed down her throat to her breasts. "I'm serious. I've got to figure out what I'm going to do with you."

"I have several suggestions for you."

"I'll just bet you do, but that was not what I meant." She tried to inject a tone of firmness and resolution into her words, but that wasn't so easy when the man had licked her nipple and was blowing on the moist tip to watch the areole crinkle. She bit back a moan. "I just found out my lover is a vampire. I've got some decisions to make."

Dmitri moved back up and draped himself over her, his bare chest pressing her into the mattress, his legs between hers, the rough fabric of his jeans teasing her naked skin. She could feel the length of his hard-on pressing against her, but it was the tender heat in his eyes that captivated her.

"*Dushka*," he murmured, using his free hand to cup her face and rubbing his thumb over her soft mouth. "I am afraid your decisions have already been made. I will not allow you to leave me. You are mine, and I intend to keep you."

"Keep me?" She blinked. "You can't just decide to keep me!"

"And who shall stop me?"

"I will!" She squirmed beneath him, trying to slide out of his embrace. Not that it did her much good. The man weighed a ton, and all of it was muscle. He controlled her easily. "I've *never* let a man tell me what I can and can't do, and I'm not about to start now, Mr. Dictator. I've got a mind and a will of my own, and I am not your possession!"

"But I have possessed you, *milaya*."

"Big frickin' whoop," she growled, still wriggling. "That doesn't give you any rights to me. I might like to let you have your way in bed, Dmitri, but outside of it is a whole 'nother story. I'm sexually submissive. I'm not a doormat."

Dmitri sighed. "I never thought of you as a doormat. And I have never treated you as one. I love your fire and your stubborn streak. I would not want to rob you of those."

His words convinced her to at least stop struggling, not that it seemed to be making any sort of impression on him anyway. "Dmitri, if you love those things about me, then how can you ask me to let you make these sorts of decisions for me?"

"Regina, how can you expect me to let you go?"

His softly spoken words and expression of weary longing almost made her melt. She nearly gave up the ghost right there, wrapped her thighs around him and called him, "sir, yes, sir." But her mind saved her, beating her heart back into its ribcage and holding it at bay until they cleared the rest of this mess up once and for all.

"Dmitri, you barely know me. We've spent a total of about twelve hours together over the course of one week. Why am I supposed to think you want me? For this?" She arched her hips against him and ignored the flash of pleasure it caused. "Somehow I don't think you have much trouble getting laid."

His eyes flashed.

"Do you think this is merely 'getting laid' to me?" he demanded, his frustration clear. "Do you think I feel this way with other women? That you would feel this way with other men? You are my mate. The woman I have never found in all my centuries of living. The one I thought I would never find. And I *will not* let you go."

That was almost good enough, Reggie acknowledged to herself over the flood of pleasure and wonder the statement caused; but almost didn't count. She wanted the whole shebang. So she prodded the wounded lion.

"Why not, Dmitri?" Self-preservation be damned. This was her future they were tap dancing around. If she had to make him furious to get what she wanted, so be it. "Why not let me go? Why not write this off as a couple of nights of good sex and move on to your next conquest? Why not let me move on? Why not let me give Marc a call and let us have a real date this time? The kind that doesn't end at the restaurant but in a bed or on the floor or in the back seat of his car. Why not?"

"Because I love you!" he roared. "And no man will *ever* touch you but me!"

A smile curved her mouth until she probably looked like an idiot. She didn't care. "Well, okay, then."

"You are going to be my wife, and I refuse to hear—" He jerked to a stop mid-tirade and blinked down at her. "What did you say?"

"I said okay, you big goob." She grinned. "I love you, too. I don't want anyone else to touch me. And incidentally, if that was a proposal—and if it was, it was a god-awful excuse for one—then the answer is yes."

"Yes?"

"Yes," she repeated and tugged impatiently at his grip, which still pinned her hands over her head to the mattress. "I'll marry you, provided you ask me again properly. And since I plan to celebrate our five-hundredth anniversary at the very least, that means you'll have to make me a vampire, too. Let's get started. I'm not really looking forward to the blood-drinking part, so do you think we could get that over with first?"

The man looked positively shell-shocked. "You want to marry me and become a vampire."

"Isn't that what I just said?" She finally tugged her hands free—or, he let her tug her hands free—and wrapped them around his neck. "Now let's hurry up before I lose my nerve. Not about the marrying part, about the vampire part. I'm really not good with blood. I faint at the sight of it. I won't have to look at blood when I drink it, will I? Because that might make things kind of tough for me…"

While she babbled, Dmitri's expression went from stunned to satisfied. When she finally trailed into silence, it shifted into its natural state—wicked.

"You may keep your eyes closed if you wish," he purred, pushing her thighs further apart and settling his hips deeper into the cradle of hers. "But if you do, you might miss something."

Reggie groaned and buried her fingers in his thick, dark hair when he lowered his head and latched onto her puckered nipple. "Oh no," she moaned. "I wouldn't want to miss a thing."

Chapter Sixteen

No man should be able to make her this horny this fast, Reggie thought while she melted under Dmitri's warm mouth and skilled fingers. And no man should be wearing his jeans while he got her this hot.

Forcing her hands to give up their compelling nest in his hair, she slid them over his shoulders and between their bodies to the button at his waistband.

Dmitri chuckled and lifted his head from her breast. "Is someone feeling impatient?"

"Someone is going to remove your jeans with her teeth if you don't get them off in the next fifteen seconds," she grumbled, already on the third button. Only one to go.

"Promises, promises," he teased. Levering himself back onto his knees, he brushed her hands away and finished the job himself, stripping away the denim and dropping it over the side of the bed.

Reggie had to take several deep breaths just to keep from screaming, "Take me!" like the heroine of a melodramatic romance novel. *Ye gods and little fishes.* Would she ever get used to the way this man looked? From the top of his tousled, black hair to the soles of his strong, bare feet, the man oozed masculine perfection. And he was all hers. She offered up a quick and fervent prayer of thanks while he prowled toward her on his hands and knees.

"Help," she whispered, a small smile curving her lips while lust darkened her eyes. "I think I'm about to be ravished by a wicked vampire. Help. Somebody please help me."

"There is no one to hear your screams, girl." He grinned at her, wicked and sexy while he forced her legs wide apart and crawled between them. "I have you at my mercy."

"And will you be merciful?" Her question made it clear mercy was the last thing she wanted. She reached out to trace a line down the center of his chest before she wrapped her hand around his erect cock.

"Not even if you beg, *milka*."

Reggie heaved a happy sigh. "Oh, good."

Dmitri chuckled and removed her hand from his cock. "You will not sway me from my intent. I will have you as I please, and you will not stop me. What do you think of that, Regina?"

She squirmed a little closer, spread her legs a little wider and grabbed onto the bottom rail of the headboard with both hands. "I think you'd better get started."

"There is much to do," he agreed and bent to kiss her.

She parted her lips willingly for him, welcoming him inside with teasing strokes of her tongue. She loved kissing him, loved when he blocked out the world with his shadow and his heat and his passion. When they kissed, she felt almost as close to him as when he buried his cock deep inside her, but instead of easing her frustration, his kiss heightened it, and she whimpered.

He drew back and surveyed her face, her eyelids heavy, her breathing rapid and shallow, her lips moist and swollen. He smiled in satisfaction and stunned her by pulling away and standing, giving her an affectionate swat on the flank. "Get up."

"What?" She frowned at him, confused and a bit miffed.

He folded his arms across his chest and gazed down at her. "If I get to ravish you without mercy this time, I have some specific ravishments in mind. So, get up."

Reggie released the bed rail and sat up abruptly. Her frown turned into a scowl. "This better be good," she grumped, sliding off the bed and stomping over to stand next to him.

"Trust me. It will be." He winked at her and climbed back onto the mattress, settling himself in a seated position with his back resting against the headboard and his legs folded Indian style in front of him. The lazy pasha-look again. Damn it if he couldn't pull it off. He patted his lap. "Come here."

Now that had possibilities.

Reggie gave up her scowl and crawled up after him, suddenly eager to play along. The man was turning her into a wanton, and boy, was it fun.

He grabbed her hips when she stopped in front of him. "Straddle me."

She obeyed with alacrity. She climbed into his lap, her legs on either side of his hips; but when she reached down to guide him into her, he grabbed her hand and guided it to his shoulder. Maintaining a one handed grip on her hip, he repeated the motion with her other hand, holding her firmly to keep her from impaling herself on his cock.

"Not yet," he scolded. "Wait until you have permission, naughty girl. I want you to keep your hands exactly where I put them. Do you understand?"

She nodded, anxious and breathless.

"Good. Now hold absolutely still."

Reggie tried, she really did. But when he released her hips and slid his hands lower, teasing them over her pussy before sliding them under her thighs, she couldn't help herself. She shivered.

Then she jumped at the sharp impact of his hand against her ass when he gave her a firm spank.

"I said still."

Reggie gulped and nodded, locking her muscles against any more involuntary movement. Not because she didn't want him to spank her again (Lord, just the thought got her juices flowing, not to mention what the reality had done to her. She had creamed all over his thigh!), but because she needed him inside her desperately, and she hoped if she obeyed, he'd get there that much faster.

"Are you going to behave?" he demanded.

She nodded and her fingers clenched on his hard shoulders.

"Good. Lift your hips."

She obeyed instantly. She rose up on her knees until her hips lifted a few inches from his and froze once again.

"Very good, *milka*."

His hands slid back between her thighs, knuckles deliberately brushing against her pussy on the way. He moved his right arm against her thigh until she would either have to disobey him and move it, or…well, she'd have to move it. The man was stronger than Godzilla. She teetered on the edge of action and consequence for a handful of seconds.

"Lift your leg and drape it over my arm," he commanded, giving her the excuse she needed.

She shifted her weight to her right knee, preparing to drape the left over his arm as he commanded. He spanked her sharply with his left hand and forced her to shift back to where she had been. She could almost feel the bright red print his hand had left on her ass.

"I only told you to move your leg," he grumbled, fixing her with a stern gaze.

"But I'm kneeling. If I move that leg, I'll fall."

"I won't let you fall, *dushka*," he assured her, "but neither will I let you disobey me. Move your leg."

Reggie did as he instructed, preparing herself to collapse in a tangled heap on top of him, but she never did. As soon as she moved her leg, simultaneously gripping his shoulders tighter for balance, he slid his arm underneath her and cupped her ass cheek in his hand, holding her safe and stable.

"Good. Now the other."

She took a deep breath, knowing the only thing she would have to rely on to hold her up was Dmitri. Of course, the man could probably hold up the leaning Tower of Pisa, so who was she to doubt him? She obeyed, lifting her right leg and feeling his arm slide underneath her on that side, as well, to grip her other ass cheek.

"Now, put your hands on top of your head and leave them there."

She did, giving up her last ounce of control. Tentatively, she gave him her weight, relaxing her body until she really was completely at his mercy.

With her knees draped over his arms, she had no control and no leverage. She couldn't move unless he moved her. She couldn't get away, couldn't get closer. All she could do was stare at him helplessly and feel her pussy growing wetter and wetter.

Dmitri must have noticed her arousal. Even if he couldn't feel her moisture, he could clearly see her nipples were as hard as little pebbles. She knew he could see that because he stared right at them, clearly appreciating the way the position he'd ordered her to assume had pushed her breasts out in front of her.

"Very nice, *milaya*," he murmured, still staring at her nipples. "So you can be a good girl when you put your mind to it. How long do you suppose you can last?"

When he flicked his tongue over her nipple and sucked the tight little bud into his mouth, she figured about five minutes. When he shifted his arms to urge her hips closer to his and nudged at her cunt with the blunt head of his cock, she revised the estimate down to about five seconds. The man was trying to kill her.

"Please, Misha," she begged, her fingers clenching in her own hair. "I need you to fuck me."

She was not going to waste time making him persuade her to say it. She wanted it *now*.

He released her nipple and nuzzled his way to her other breast. "You say that so prettily, *milka*. How could I deny you?"

Reggie had no idea and no desire to find out. Thankfully, he didn't make her. His fingers tightened on her ass, and she felt the muscles in his arms bunch and shift while he lowered her slowly onto his erection, so slowly she counted each separate inch when he fed it to her. She gasped out a tortured moan. In this position, he felt enormous, as shockingly huge as the first time. Again pleasure warred with pain while her cunt attempted to stretch to accommodate his length and thickness.

"Oh, God," she moaned. "Wait, Misha! Wait, wait, wait."

"No," he growled. "You will take me, *milaya*. I need you to take me. Relax for me."

She shuddered, wishing it were that easy, but there was nothing easy about this. Biting down hard on her lower lip, she forced her muscles to make room for him, all the while wishing she could force herself down on him. If she could get it over with quickly, like ripping off a band-aid, she knew her body would adjust, but he held all the leverage. As he lowered her onto his cock, she became more and more powerless. While he lowered her hips, he simultaneously shifted his arms, forcing her thighs to lift and bend further toward her body. When he finally hilted in her, she was bent almost in two. If she moved her legs another couple of inches, she could rest her ankles on his shoulders. She didn't move, though. She simply sat there, impaled on his cock, still and tense and obedient.

Misha arched his hips beneath her, ensuring not a centimeter of his flesh remained outside of her body. With a loud groan, he clenched his hands on her ass, his fingers digging deeply into the tender cleft while he buried his face in the curve of her neck. "God, you feel so good around me, *dushka*. Your cunt is so sweet and tight, and so wet for me."

His words seemed almost as erotic as his possession of her, and her pussy contracted in response. She moaned.

"What do you feel, *milaya*?" he demanded, lifting her a few inches so he could feel the pleasure of thrusting into her again. "What do you feel when I am inside you?"

"You, Misha," she panted, helplessly taking him while he established a slow, heavy thrusting rhythm, lifting her off his cock and slamming her hips back down. "You're all I feel. All I think of. God, you're all I know."

Misha groaned his reaction and increased the speed of his thrusts until Reggie's breasts bounced up and down with every impact. She saw his eyes fix on them before he leaned forward and took one nipple, still red from his attention earlier, and sucked hard.

Reggie cried out, and her body arched helplessly closer, demanding more. The pressure of his mouth increased, became almost painful, and Reggie gloried in it. She gloried in everything he did to her, every touch, every kiss, every thrust of his cock. She loved the way his teeth tugged at her nipple and his fingers bit into her ass. She'd even loved his hard slaps when he'd spanked her. She wanted everything he had to give her. She wanted him.

"Misha!" she shouted when her control snapped, and she wrapped her arms around him, pulling him closer, as if she could crawl inside his skin. "Misha, I love you so much." She shouted it, whimpered it, moaned it, while she came, the pleasure making her mindless and desperate.

That was the end of it. The words, ones that overwhelmed him with joy, snapped his tattered control, and he spun her around until she lay beneath him. Hooking his arms under her knees, he pressed her legs back against her body and thrust into her like an animal. He fucked her as if it were the end of the world, and she lay beneath him, fists clenching in the sheets until they tore, helpless to do anything but take him and revel in his savagery.

He pumped into her, filling her with his come, and while he drained himself into her tight pussy, he sank his fangs into the blue vein that ran through her breast to her areole and he drank her blood from her nipple.

Chapter Seventeen

I think I passed out. I think he fucked me until I passed out.
I fucked you until we both passed out.

He nuzzled her breast and planted a soft kiss on her tender nipple, the one he'd fed from. He laid sprawled half on top of her, his weight pinning her in place. He seemed absolutely disinclined to move. Frankly, Reggie couldn't blame him. Staying right where they were sounded pretty damned good to her, too.

A smug, and probably goofy, grin curved her mouth. "Yeah. And it was fantastic."

Dmitri chuckled. "I'm glad you enjoyed it, *dushka*, because I don't think I will be capable again for at least half a century."

Reggie tickled his ear with her finger and hooked one leg over his hip. Her grin turned wicked. "Wanna try for half an hour?"

This time, he laughed straight out, and the rumbling noise shook the bed. "You are an optimist. It is impossible."

Her hand slid down his back and between his thighs to tickle his scrotum.

He amended his opinion. "Highly unlikely."

She squeezed gently.

"Almost inevitable."

Reggie laughed.

"Enough, wench," Misha growled, levering off of her and sitting up to once again lean against the headboard. When he pulled her into his lap, Reggie winced.

"Not, this way again," she protested. "My hips are still too sore from last time."

"As flattering as your confidence in me is," he laughed, "your reprieve will last a while longer. We have other matters to tend to than our bodies' cravings for each other."

Reggie blinked. "We do?"

"We do. You have agreed to marry me, Regina. Do not tell me you've forgotten already."

She grinned at his expression of mock disapproval. "Well, I admit I was distracted, but no, I remember." She kissed his firm lips. "I may even be looking forward to it."

"And you asked me to turn you into a vampire." His dark eyes searched her expression.

Reggie made it easy for him and grimaced. "Not so looking forward to that part."

Dmitri hugged her close and stroked her back with soothing motions. "You do not have to do this, *dushka*. It is not necessary. We can manage quite well if you wish to remain human."

Realizing what a silly git she'd be to turn down a man who was that hot in bed *and* gave a damn or two about her feelings, Reggie shook her head and raised a determinedly cheerful face to him. "And let you go off chasing after sweet young things as soon as I start wrinkling?" she teased. "Not a chance. Like I said, I want a five-hundredth anniversary. What is that? Raw platinum? What comes after silver, gold and diamond?"

He grinned as if her answer pleased him. "I am entirely unsure, however it would be my pleasure to discover this with you."

He kissed her soundly and left her perched in bemusement on his lap while he reached into the nightstand drawer and pulled out a sheathed dagger.

"Because you do not yet have fangs," he explained. He pulled off the protective leather, and her eyes widened.

That looks awfully sharp…

He cupped her chin in his hand and forced her gaze to shift from the knife to his face. "You do not have to do this," he repeated with firm authority. "It is forever, *milka*, and I would rather lose you than have you come to hate me."

Somehow, the freedom of that choice made her decision to bind herself to him all that much more definite. She kissed him tenderly, lingering over it, showing him without words how much she loved him and how much she wanted to be with him always.

When she pulled back, her expression held warmth and love and humor. "Forever may not be long enough for me," she warned him, half teasing. "I might follow you into the after life. Maybe *you* should think twice about this."

"You would not have to follow me. I would not go without you, *dushka*."

Reggie smiled, her nerves giving way to a sense of peace and excitement. "Then let's get this done, bucko, before you decide to back out. What do I need to do?"

He searched her face one last time before nodding, apparently content with what he'd read there. "As I said, you will have to drink from me. I will make a small cut in my flesh. You will have to drink the blood from it."

"Do I need to drink a lot?" She was willing to do this, wanted to do this, even, but the idea still seemed a little creepy.

"Not a vast quantity, but enough to set the transformation in motion. You will know when it has begun."

"Will it hurt?"

"It is a…peculiar sensation, but you should not find it too painful."

Reggie absorbed that, paused a moment, and nodded decisively. "Okay. I'm ready."

He smiled at her and before she could blink, he raised the dagger and sliced a narrow cut in his chest above his heart. She couldn't see it at first, but he leaned over to put the dagger back in the drawer and when he faced her again, blood had begun to seep from the wound, dark and thick against his skin.

Reggie bit her lip and looked uncertain.

"Your choice, *dushka*. Either way, I will love you always."

She took a deep breath, inhaling the masculine scent of him along with the scent of sex, and knew he meant it. "Good," she whispered, "because you're never getting away from me now."

She lowered her head, feeling time stretch around her into slow motion. The first drop of blood worked its way free of the welling fluid and trickled down his chest. Reggie got to it just as it reached his nipple. She captured it with her tongue, caressing him while she did so. He tasted familiar and foreign, dark and rich and coppery, like himself, sweeter than his come, saltier than his mouth. She found the flavor intriguing.

She traced the crimson path back up his chest to the wound and dragged her tongue along the length of the cut, cleaning it of the accumulated blood. More welled up in its place, and, when the first drops slid easily down her throat, she realized she wanted more. The flavor of him changed even while she sucked the first mouthful from his wound. It became sweeter and smoother, like some rare liquor. The coppery taste of blood faded, and she found she could savor him like wine. She purred deep in her throat and snuggled closer while she began to drink from him in truth.

He went to her head and made her drunk with the taste of him. She couldn't get close enough to him. Even when he wrapped his arms around her and rolled onto his side, bringing her with him, she wanted more. She wanted to merge with him, to crawl inside him and rest beneath his skin beside his heart. She hooked her leg over his hip and pressed her hips against him, sucking hungrily from his chest. She felt so thirsty, and he was the only thing that could quench her need.

She existed in a black haze, all the world muffled but for her senses, which were acute. She gloried in the texture of his skin and hair, tasted his blood, smelled his scent and wanted him. She heard him moan somewhere above her, and his hand clenched on her thigh and raised it higher. The thick length of him probed at her tender opening and slid deep.

It overwhelmed her. She sank her teeth into his skin, unaware they had lengthened and sharpened while she fed. She pulled him closer with newfound strength, meeting his every thrust when he began to surge into her.

She'd never felt anything like this. Before, when Misha had fucked her, he'd been the center of her universe. Now, he was the center of *the* universe, and she wanted to weep and howl with the joy of it. Instead she drank deeply and moaned against his skin when he bowed his head and sank his fangs deep into her neck. He drank back the blood she was taking, and passion and power arced between them, a never-ending chain of pleasure and heat and lust and love.

The tension broke over them simultaneously, her cunt milking his cock while he pulsed his release inside of her. She tore her mouth away from his chest and screamed, a banshee sound of ecstasy and transformation. He echoed her with an animal roar of pleasure and triumph. They melted together in a tangled heap of blood and sex and sweat.

When Reggie finally managed to stir a long time later, she realized there really wasn't any blood. Like he'd said, the wounds seemed to have closed even while they'd pulled away from each other. But there was plenty of sweat and plenty of sex.

Reggie wrinkled her nose. "I need a shower."

For some reason, Dmitri found that vastly amusing. He laughed out loud and hugged her close. "I love you, *dushka*. You delight me."

"I'd delight you more if I didn't stink," she said. She sniffed and arched an eyebrow at him. "In fact, I think you'd delight me more if you—"

Dmitri glared at her, though his eyes glinted with humor. "Do not insult me by telling me I stink, Regina Elaina. I may have changed you, but I am still the one in charge here."

"Yeah, yeah. You're the great big alpha-male, O Exalted One," she said, pushing at his shoulders until he rolled away from her. "But I am going to take a shower. Turning into a vampire takes a lot out of a girl. Which door leads to the—"

Her chatter ground to an abrupt halt, and Reggie fell back to the bed with a muffled thump. "Oh, wow. I almost forgot. I'm a vampire."

Dmitri surveyed her dazed look with humor. "Almost. It will take a few more hours for the transformation to complete itself, but you are on your way."

"What do you mean, 'almost'?" she demanded, glaring at him. "I drank blood. I had fangs!"

"Those are merely the first stage," he dismissed, sitting up on the edge of the bed and scratching his chest absently. "In a few hours you will also have excellent night vision, amazing strength, acute hearing and incredible speed. You're not done yet."

That took the wind out of her sails. "Oh."

She thought for a second, and when she looked back at him, she looked like she was plotting something. "Will I get as strong as you?"

He laughed out loud. "Not a chance." She pouted, and he kissed the tip of her nose. "Not only am I seven hundred and thirty-two years older than you, *dushka*, but I am also a man. Even among our kind, nature has weighted the advantage with men when it comes to strength."

Reggie humphed and stood, heading for the door she thought might lead to the bathroom. "Then I guess if it's just like being human, nature compensated by giving women the advantage when it comes to intelligence."

She punctuated her comment by looking back at him over her shoulder and sticking out her tongue. Clearly, she had maturity on her side, too.

Dmitri gave a mock growl and started after her, but the thunderous clap of the door slamming back against the wall stopped both of them in their tracks.

"Get away from her, you dirty blood sucker, before I turn you into vampire shish-kabob!"

Chapter Eighteen

It took Reggie a few seconds to pull her mouth closed, but the sight of your four best friends bursting through your lover's bedroom door, brandishing crosses and sharpened broom handles, can really shake a girl up.

Danice stepped warily forward to stand beside Ava, a makeshift cross, fashioned from two rulers and some duct tape, held out in front of her. Corinne and Missy stepped into the room and took positions flanking them.

"Come on, Reg," Danice urged, her voice soft and soothing, as if she were talking to a child or a victim of some violent crime. "We're here for you. It'll all be okay now. Just come here to me, and we'll get you out of here. Poor baby."

Reggie just stared at her. "Are you out of your minds? What the hell are you doing here?"

"I believe this is the cavalry, *dushka*. Your friends have come to rescue you from my evil, blood sucking clutches." Dmitri's voice showed exactly how amusing he found the situation. Reggie glanced in his direction and saw him leaning unconcerned up against the bedpost, his arms crossed over his muscular chest and his legs crossed at the ankles. His very bare legs, since he was still completely naked.

And so was she.

"Jeez, guys! Could you maybe knock next time? We're not exactly dressed for company here." Grumbling all the way, Reggie stalked back toward the bed, yanked off a sheet and wrapped it around her in a makeshift toga.

When Dmitri made no move to cover himself, she grabbed a pillow and threw it at him.

He caught it and grinned.

"I think he must be using some sort of mind control on her. What do we do now?"

Corrine whispered her theory, but Reggie heard it with no trouble. Her hearing had already improved.

"Dmitri is not controlling my mind, you idiot! And none of you have to do a bloody thing except apologize for barging in on us uninvited and then get the hell out of here so we can get dressed."

Ava ignored her friend's scowl and stepped forward, holding an intricate gilded crucifix toward Dmitri. "We're not leaving without you, Reggie. We know all about your new lover. He wasn't just at that Goth party for kicks. He's a real vampire. You're not safe with him."

"You're out of your mind!"

"No, Reggie, it's true!" Missy, clutching her own cross, moved closer to Regina, her face an earnest picture of concern. "I thought she was crazy, too, at first. But then what she told us started to make sense. Did you know the only recorded photos of Vidâme's ancestors are of adult eldest sons? No mothers, no fathers, no children, no old people. Just men in their thirties who manage to look almost exactly alike."

Reggie started to open her mouth to berate some sense into her friends, but Danice stopped her.

"It's the truth! It's freaky, Reg. Every single picture could be this guy's twin, and in all the photos, the dude is only ever seen at night!" Danice shuddered.

"And what about that hickey on your neck, Reg?" Corinne joined in. "Danice was right all along. It was a bite mark. This monster drank your blood. I'm telling you, he's a vampire!"

"And I'm telling you, I know!"

Reggie's shout cut straight through her friends' protests and even made Dmitri quirk an eyebrow. Reggie thought about smacking the smirk right off his face, but she refused to resort to violence. No matter how good it sounded. She contented herself with glaring at him and snarling before she turned back toward her friends.

Ava took one look at Reggie's expression and stiffened. Corinne screamed and Missy looked ready to faint. Danice jumped back until she hit the wall, and Ava turned her cross toward her friend.

"God, Regina, I'm so sorry," Ava whispered, a mask of agony twisting her features. "We came as soon as I heard from Marc that you'd been kidnapped from the restaurant. But we're too late. He turned you into one of them."

"How do you know that?" Reggie demanded. Ava's reaction kind of hurt her feelings.

"Your fangs," Dmitri explained, dropping the pillow and crossing to Regina's side to wrap his arm around her shoulders. He paid no attention to the cross-wielding reactions of her friends. "You became angry, *dushka*, and your fangs emerged. It is an emotional reaction you will learn to control."

"Yeah, and I hope you'll keep that in mind right about now. That whole control over your emotions thing." Graham appeared in the doorway, looking sheepish. He shrugged to Dmitri. "I did the best I could."

Reggie threw her hands up in the air and turned on Dmitri. "Great! Now we're having a party in your bedroom! Did you invite the neighbors, or just your closest vampire buddies?"

Dmitri spared her an impatient glance before glaring at the new intruder. "Graham is not a vampire. He's a werewolf, and I did not invite him at all. In fact, I assumed he would be keeping an eye on your friends and preventing this very event from occurring."

"Give me a break, Misha," Graham said, stepping into the room with a belligerent expression. The four human women scattered out of his path. "I'd like to see you try and ride herd on four humans with estrogen poisoning. They're royal pains. They almost made Rafe want to kick my ass for talking him into helping me with them."

"Actually, I would like very much to kick your ass for that." Another male voice drifted in from the hall a second before an unfamiliar, dark-haired man stepped into the crowded bedroom.

Reggie uttered a choked scream. "Is this another werewolf you didn't invite? Should I expect the entire uninvited population of Manhattan to join us next? Are we supposed to serve refreshments?"

"Werecat," Rafe corrected with a lazy smile. "I'm not a wolf, but lycanthrope is a great nonspecific term that's guaranteed not to offend any of us. And I'm Rafael De Santos. Pleased to meet you."

Regina reflexively shook the hand he extended to her before she remembered how furious this entire farce had made her. She snatched her hand back and used it to poke Dmitri hard in the shoulder. "This is all your fault!"

"What is all my fault?" Dmitri looked offended.

"Everything," she proclaimed. "The fact that I'm losing my mind. The fact that my friends have already lost their minds. The fact that I have half the world in my bedroom, and I just got turned into a vampire. I'm sure global warming is your fault, too. I'm just not sure how yet."

"Don't forget the fact that he scared your friends so badly, they're hiding behind the bed," Rafe offered with a grin.

Reggie turned around and saw her friends peering warily over the mattress from the other side of Dmitri's massive bed. She rolled her eyes.

"Actually, that's the one thing I can blame on you two," she said, extending her glare to encompass Graham as well. "They were fine until you showed up. You're the ones they're scared of."

"We're not the ones they were waving crosses at," Graham said. "I think that means they're afraid of you."

"Ha! My friends know me better than that."

Determined to prove her point—since her life couldn't get much more surreal than it had in the past ten minutes—Reggie stalked over to the other side of the bed, and grabbed the crosses and broom handles out of her friends' hands so quickly, they couldn't even think to protest. She grabbed the woman closest to her—Danice— and gave her a great big hug and a smacking kiss on her cheek.

"See? My friends know I would never hurt them. They're intelligent, modern women who don't fall pray to superstitions."

From the corner of her eye, Reggie caught a glimpse of Corinne's hand sneaking out toward a cross. She reached out casually and planted her foot on it.

"They know crosses and garlic and holy water are nonsense, and vampires are not evil demons from the depths of hell." She ignored the shocked expressions on the faces of her friends and continued. "They also know if I didn't have complete faith in Dmitri, I would never be with him, and that I'm a grown woman fully capable of making my own decisions about who I want to date and who I want to marry."

"Marry?" Ava almost choked on the word.

"And they know that even if I did become a vampire, I'm still the same person I always was, and I still love them as much as I did before. And they know they're not getting out of being the bridesmaids at my wedding, so they might as well get used to the idea!"

By the time Reggie finished her tirade, she was panting, her friends were reeling, and Rafe and Graham were looking chastened.

Dmitri laughed.

"Well, I think you have explained everything to everyone's satisfaction, *dushka*," he said, pulling her into his arms. "I believe they are only waiting for us to set the date."

"Don't think you're off scot-free, mister," she grumbled, glaring up at him. "You just stood there buck naked and flashed all that manly muscle at my friends. It's indecent! Would you go put some clothes on?"

He threw back his head and laughed harder. "Why should I?" he teased her. "Our guests are on their way out, and I will just have to strip them off again, because I intend to make love to you as soon as we are alone."

Reggie scowled. "You know what they say about good intentions."

"That refers only to the good ones. I intend to be very wicked, *dushka*."

"Um, I think that's our cue to leave," Corinne said, breaking the tension and dragging herself up to stand on shaky legs. "It's…been a really long night."

Reggie dragged her eyes from Dmitri. "You don't have to go. I'm sorry I yelled like that. I was just a little tense. But you could hang out for a while. I could get you guys something to eat."

Ava turned green and shook her head frantically.

"Oh, don't be such an idiot," Reggie said, rolling her eyes. "I meant I'd call for pizza or something. I just had a drink. I'm not going to snack on my bridesmaids."

Missy stepped forward bravely and gave Reggie a hug. "We know that, Reg. It's just going to take a little getting used to. Give us a few days, and I'm sure we'll be fine."

With the last of her anger faded away, Reggie realized she was nervous. What if her friends couldn't accept what she had become? What would she do?

But when she looked into Missy's eyes, she saw the other woman meant every word. Yes, Missy was a bit shell shocked, but her love for her friend was stronger than her fear. Looking around at the other women, Reggie saw the same truth reflected in each of them. It really would be okay.

Chapter Nineteen

It took a while to clear out the circus in Dmitri's bedroom, but they finally managed it around four that morning. There were a few cacophonous minutes of questions, explanations and discussions where Reggie demanded to know how her friends had managed to research vampires, evade trailing werewolves and take up breaking and entering. She also wanted to know how they'd accomplished all that, but couldn't remember to knock before barging into someone's bedroom. Dmitri expressed admiration—or maybe that had been fear—when Ava explained how she'd will-powered her way past his mind games, shimmied out her eighteen-inch-square basement window right under Graham's nose, and gathered up an impromptu army for the cavalry charge.

He also took the opportunity to reemphasize that whole "knocking" thing.

Reggie sat on the side of the bed and heard bits of the conversation that took place when Dmitri escorted his two friends to the front door. It seemed like her hearing was improving by the minute, and a shiver of excitement passed through her. All of a sudden the possibilities open to her in her new life sounded exciting. Letting Dmitri turn her no longer felt like even a minor sacrifice. It felt like a blessing. Tentatively, she reached out with fumbling, infant senses and tried to share some of her new feelings with Dmitri.

She knew the instant he sensed her, knew his pleasure and his affection.

If you wish to take a shower, you should do so now. His voice rumbled in her head, a thousand times clearer and sharper than she'd ever heard it. It left her breathless. *It will be dawn soon, and at the beginning, the sunrise will exhaust you. I will be up in a minute.*

Grinning, she decided to take his advice and headed for the bathroom, or at least for the door she thought probably led to the bathroom. Dmitri still hadn't given her the tour.

She guessed correctly, and felt quite pleased with herself when she turned on the shower. She had barely stepped under the spray before he crowded in with her. Not that he needed to crowd. The shower — and the bathroom — was just as spacious and elegant as the rest of his house. Still, she ignored him while she reached for the bottle of shampoo on the shelf and lathered her hair, but she couldn't ignore him when he slipped his hands into the foamy cap and massaged her scalp with strong, gentle fingers. She gave in and leaned back against his chest on a blissful moan.

"You should call into work," he murmured while he continued to rub lazy circles in her hair. "After your change, you will need to sleep for most of the day."

"I already took the day off."

His fingers paused then resumed. "I am going to pretend you did so because you expected me to rescue you from your date. Otherwise, I would have to punish you."

He tugged gently on her hair and leaned down to nip her shoulder.

Reggie grinned, and purred her reply, pressing her hips back against him. "Oh, no. Please don't hurt me."

Dmitri chuckled. "That is good, though," he continued. "It gives us all of tomorrow evening and the entire weekend to move your things out of your apartment."

Reggie stiffened. "I'm moving out of my apartment?"

He turned her around and tilted her head back to wash the soap out of her hair. "You have agreed to marry me. That means we will live together."

She jerked her head up and glared at him. "But you're just assuming I'll be the one to move. I just got through yelling like a fishwife at a bunch of people who were making assumptions about me, Dmitri. Don't get me started again. I told you before, just because I'm submissive in bed doesn't mean that—"

Dmitri chuckled and picked up a bar of soap. "I am not trying to run your life, *katyonak*. You may sheath your claws. But your apartment is too small for both of us. My house is much larger and more private. It is also owned and not rented, so it is much safer for both of us. I was being logical, not dictatorial."

Reggie eyed him warily, but couldn't really argue with his reasoning. "I guess you're right. But you'd better be careful with that, Misha. I'm not going to become some plaything. I'm going to be your wife. That means an equal partner."

He slid his soapy hands up over her breasts and squeezed. "I am always careful with you, *dushka*," he purred even as he slid one hand down to cup her between her thighs. "And I do not think of you as a thing, even though I very much enjoy playing with you."

He slipped his fingers into her pussy, and she laughed around her moan. "Misha, you can't always end our discussions with sex."

"Then do not bore me with discussion when I am hungry for you." He twisted his hand and rubbed his thumb over her clit. "We will make each other happy, *milaya*. What else is there to discuss?"

It took every ounce of her strength and determination to articulate anything beyond a plea for more sex, but Reggie managed it. Barely.

"What about my job?" she demanded, grabbing his wrist in both hands to hold it still. "How am I supposed to go to work if I'm going to be sleeping all day long?"

Misha sighed and withdrew his fingers, reaching for the soap again and lathering her legs. "You could manage it if you wanted, with a lot of effort," he grumbled. "But there is no need for you to work if you do not wish it. As you guessed this evening, I am disgustingly wealthy. I can well afford to keep you for eternity."

Her eyes narrow warningly. "Misha, you're not thinking of telling me I can't work, are you? Because —"

"Regina! I said it before. The only thing I will forbid you to do is to leave me. Other than that, you may do as you please. I want to make you happy. As happy as you make me. Whatever you want, I will give to you. Wherever you wish to go, I will take you. If you wish to work, you may. If you wish not to work, you may. You may do anything you want." He paused. "Except sleep with another man. Or touch another man. Just to be safe, you should probably not look at any other man."

Reggie laughed and threw her arms around him, hugging him close while the very last of her fears washed down the drain. She peppered his face with kisses, feeling a sense of exaltation fill her to overflowing. She wanted to dance and sing and laugh and cry and yell for joy. But most of all, she just wanted Misha.

"You never need to worry about that, my darling, jealous, vampiric Misha." She hugged him tight and pulled herself up his chest, wrapping her legs around his hips and kissing him passionately. "You are the only man I want. The only man I will ever want. Why should I ever need anything else when I have you?"

He smiled at her, the small, wicked grin she had grown to love. "You do have me, *dushka*. You will always have me."

"And you have me, Misha. Forever."

"Forever," he echoed and lowered his mouth to hers. They kissed until the water threatened to turn cold and they had both turned very hot indeed. Misha switched off the water without dislodging Reggie from her position around his waist and carried her back to the bedroom.

He tumbled her down onto the tousled sheets and kissed her again, his hunger making his intent more than clear. At his urging, Reggie loosened her grip around his waist so he could slide down her body and take a taut nipple between his lips. She smiled up at the ceiling and hummed her pleasure.

"You know," she murmured, running her fingers through his thick hair, "if I'm going to be around for a few more centuries than I expected, I'm sure there are some things you'll need to teach me. After all, I've never been a vampire before."

Dmitri grunted and moved to her other breast. Reggie grinned and pulled his face up to hers for a long, deep kiss. When they were both breathless and needy and desperate to come together, she pushed him onto his back and slithered down the mattress to lick his nipples and tease his navel with her tongue.

"Just as an example, I'm sure there are nuances to drinking blood I've never considered before," she purred, gazing at him from beneath her lashes and smiling wickedly. "For instance, I'm sure it's easiest to drink from someplace that has a strong...pulse."

She closed her hand around his throbbing cock and squeezed. "If I'm going to feed on blood from now on, I should probably know the best ways to...sate my appetite."

Her tongue caressed the length of him, and he shuddered. She smiled and slid further down the bed until she was eye level with his rampant erection.

"Misha?"

"Yes, *milaya*?"

"I think I'm hungry right now," she whispered, tasting his cock like a midnight snack.

"I will always provide for you." Dmitri buried his hands in her hair and guided her mouth to him. "If you hunger, *dushka*, you should drink."

Reggie parted her smiling lips and took him into her mouth. Then she drank.

The End

About the author:

Christine Warren welcomes mail from readers. You can write to her c/o Ellora's Cave Publishing at P.O. Box 787, Hudson, Ohio 44236-0787.

Also by CHRISTINE WARREN:

- Fur Factor
- Faer Fetched
- Fighting Faer
- Pleasure Quest anthology with Marilyn Lee & Mary Winter

Why an electronic book?

We live in the Information Age — an exciting time in the history of human civilization in which technology rules supreme and continues to progress in leaps and bounds every minute of every hour of every day. For a multitude of reasons, more and more avid literary fans are opting to purchase e-books instead of paperbacks. The question to those not yet initiated to the world of electronic reading is simply: *why?*

1. *Price*. An electronic title at Ellora's Cave Publishing runs anywhere from 40-75% less than the cover price of the <u>exact same title</u> in paperback format. Why? Cold mathematics. It is less expensive to publish an e-book than it is to publish a paperback, so the savings are passed along to the consumer.

2. *Space*. Running out of room to house your paperback books? That is one worry you will never have with electronic novels. For a low one-time cost, you can purchase a handheld computer designed specifically for e-reading purposes. Many e-readers are larger than the average handheld, giving you plenty of screen room. Better yet, hundreds of titles can be stored within your new library — a single microchip. (Please note that Ellora's Cave does not endorse any specific brands. You can check our website at www.ellorascave.com for customer recommendations we make available to new consumers.)

3. *Mobility.* Because your new library now consists of only a microchip, your entire cache of books can be taken with you wherever you go.

4. *Personal preferences are accounted for.* Are the words you are currently reading too small? Too large? Too...**ANNOYING**? Paperback books cannot be modified according to personal preferences, but e-books can.

5. *Innovation.* The way you read a book is not the only advancement the Information Age has gifted the literary community with. There is also the factor of what you can read. Ellora's Cave Publishing will be introducing a new line of interactive titles that are available in e-book format only.

6. *Instant gratification.* Is it the middle of the night and all the bookstores are closed? Are you tired of waiting days—sometimes weeks—for online and offline bookstores to ship the novels you bought? Ellora's Cave Publishing sells instantaneous downloads 24 hours a day, 7 days a week, 365 days a year. Our e-book delivery system is 100% automated, meaning your order is filled as soon as you pay for it.

Those are a few of the top reasons why electronic novels are displacing paperbacks for many an avid reader. As always, Ellora's Cave Publishing welcomes your questions and comments. We invite you to email us at service@ellorascave.com or write to us directly at: P.O. Box 787, Hudson, Ohio 44236-0787.